ST. MARTIN'S

MINOTAUR

MYSTERIES

OTHER TITLES FROM ST. MARTIN'S
MINOTAUR MYSTERIES

St. Martin's Paperbacks is also proud to present
these mystery classics by Ngaio Marsh

ST. MARTIN'S PAPERBACKS TITLES
BY ROBIN HATHAWAY

The Doctor Digs a Grave

The Doctor Make a Dollhouse Call

The DOCTOR MAKES A DOLLHOUSE CALL

ROBIN HATHAWAY

St. Martin's Paperbacks

THE DOCTOR MAKES A DOLLHOUSE CALL

Copyright © 2000 by Robin Hathaway.

ISBN: 0-312-97493-0

Printed in the United States of America

St. Martin's Press hardcover edition / January 2000
St. Martin's Paperbacks edition / December 2000

St. Martin's Paperbacks are published by St. Martin's Press, 175 Fifth Avenue, New York, N.Y. 10010.

10 9 8 7 6 5 4 3 2 1

To Julie and Anne, who also love dollhouses

ACKNOWLEDGMENTS

Robert Alan Keisman, M.D., for his tireless assistance with the cardiologic aspects of this novel.

Ruth Cavin, for her excellent editing, patience, and unfailing good humor.

Laura Langlie, for being such a helpful agent and considerate friend.

Corinne R. Roxby, for sharing her library and vast knowledge of the world of miniatures.

John Parker, M.D., for his excellent advice on psychiatric matters.

Marika Rohn, for her friendship and for being there in times of crisis.

Stephanie M. Patterson, for her expert knowledge of teenage psychology.

Susan Weinstein, for her generous help and advice.

Julie and Anne Keisman, for their careful reading and critiques.

The Museum of the City of New York, for its magnificent dollhouse collection.

Once upon a time there was a very beautiful doll's house . . .
—*The Tale of Two Bad Mice* by Beatrix Potter

CHAPTER 1

November

"Judith, was that a car?" Emily no longer trusted her hearing.

"I believe it was. Oh, Emily, will you let them in? I have to check the turkey."

The two sisters, Emily and Judith Pancoast, were preparing Thanksgiving dinner for the rest of the Pancoast family, which was about to descend on them. They did this every year. It was a family tradition. And even though they were getting older—Emily eighty-two and Judith seventy-nine—it never occurred to either of them to ask the rest of the family to help. (And it never occurred to the rest of the family to offer.)

Emily looked out the front window and down the street toward the village of Seacrest. Not a car in sight. False alarm. She turned back to the parlor and glanced around. Everything was in place, just as it had been for the past one hundred years. The china shepherdess smiled pertly at the conch shell on the glass-topped mahogany table. The lace antimacassars gleamed snow white on the backs and arms of the overstuffed chairs.

And the thick volume, *Songs for the Holidays,* lay on the music rack above the piano, waiting to be flipped open to the "Thanksgiving Hymn."

We gather together
to ask the Lord's blessing . . .

Emily hummed the familiar tune as she made her way down the hall. When she came to the dollhouse, standing in its place of honor at the base of the stairwell, she paused as she always did and peered inside. The miniature parlor was just as it should be—an exact replica of the real parlor she had inspected a minute ago—down to the tiny songbook open on the music rack. But when her eyes moved on to the dining room, she gasped and felt a sharp pain in her chest. "Judith!" she cried. "Come quick!"

Judith came rushing out of the kitchen, wiping her hands on her apron. "Are they here?"

"No." Emily pointed at the dollhouse. "Look."

Judith looked. The miniature dining room table, which they had meticulously set the night before to exactly match the setting of the large table in the real dining room, was in total disarray. The china and silverware were scattered every which way. Many of the tiny, neatly rolled linen napkins were on the floor. The crisp brown turkey was upside down. And the Pamela doll, the one that resembled their niece by the same name, had fallen off its chair and lay face down on the carpet.

The sisters stared at each other.

"Who . . . ?" Emily began.

"Mice?" Judith suggested.

Emily's face relaxed. "Of course."

Once before, mice had invaded the dollhouse and eaten all the play food because it was made of salt dough, which they love. Since then the sisters had switched to a synthetic concoction called polymer. It must have been something else that attracted them.

"Oh, dear." Judith frowned. "That means traps."

"Oh, must we?" Emily looked anxious.

Again, they stared at each other in dismay. Both sisters were fond of Beatrix Potter's *The Tale of Two Bad Mice,* and they hated traps.

"We'll ask Edgar to do it," Judith said firmly.

The doorbell rang.

Judith hastily put the small dining room back in order, while Emily went to answer the door.

Emily looked through the frosted glass panel, but all she saw was a bunch of giant yellow chrysanthemums. As soon as she opened the door, Edgar poked his head around the plant and cried, "Happy Thanksgiving!"

Edgar was the younger brother of Emily and Judith, by fifteen years. Because their mother had died when he was born, the two sisters had helped raise Edgar and they were devoted to him. His bow tie, a trademark he had adopted in college and never relinquished, was a seasonal pumpkin orange. Today, it was slightly askew. His two sisters (by now, Judith had joined them) gently fought to adjust it.

"Here, stop you two," Edgar laughed. "I'll drop this plant."

"I'll take the plant," said Marie, coming up behind him.

3

When Edgar had married Marie, it had been the talk of Seacrest. The aristocratic Edgar marrying the daughter of a poor itinerant artist. But her pretty face and cheerful disposition had soon captured them all. Even their father, Captain Caleb Pancoast IV, the crotchety seaman, had been won over by her.

After hugging Marie, the sisters drew the couple inside.

"Where are the children?" asked Marie, looking around. Edgar and Marie had three children: Tom, Pamela, and Susanne. They were all grown now, but to a mother, her offspring are always "the children."

"They aren't here yet," Emily said.

"You're the first to arrive," Judith said, ushering them into the parlor.

Emily had no sooner deposited their coats, scarves, hats, and gloves in the hall closet, when the bell rang again. She had no trouble hearing its harsh clamor. (Neither sister would dream of replacing the old bell with newer, more melodious chimes.)

This time it was their nephew, Tom Pancoast, and his family. Tom had once played fullback for Brown, but today instead of a pigskin he had a folded Pack 'n Play tucked under one arm and a canvas bag bulging with baby paraphernalia over his shoulder. His wife, Mildred, held the baby. Molly and Tommy Junior, both husky children who took after their father, accepted a brief kiss from the aunts before rushing pell-mell down the hall to the dollhouse.

"Let me have the baby while you take off your coat," Judith offered.

"Thanks. Careful though," Mildred warned as she handed him over, "he's getting heavy."

"Nonsense. My, what a big boy," Judith crooned as she cuddled him.

Removing her coat, Mildred revealed a startling ensemble of purple and gold lamé. Her long dark hair hung free, and large gold hoops flashed among the strands. Fearful of the tag "housewife," she always dressed with a dramatic flair—as if she had just blown off Broadway.

Emily stowed their coats deep in the closet. Tom stashed his baby burdens in the hall and made his way to the parlor where he knew there would be sherry—the only alcohol the aunts ever supplied. The two older children ordered their mother over to the dollhouse.

"Look, Mommy—a pumpkin," Molly cried.

"And a turkey," Tommy Junior shouted.

Again the doorbell. This time it was the Turners. Adam and Susanne. Susanne was the youngest niece. Her honey-colored hair fell loosely over her tweed coat collar and her dark eyes sparkled.

"We've brought you a present." She handed Judith a tiny package wrapped in tissue paper. Amanda and Tad, her two children, watched expectantly as Judith opened it.

"Oh, my," Judith exclaimed, holding up a tiny cluster of Indian corn tied with gold ribbon.

"How nice," Emily said.

Judith carried the corn over to the dollhouse and attached it carefully to the front door just above the brass knocker.

Returning to the vestibule, the aunts greeted Susanne's husband, Adam, who had quietly followed his family inside. Adam was their favorite nephew-in-law. A physics teacher at a local boys' school, he was also a handy carpenter, plumber, and electrician. It was he who often helped them with emergency household repairs when Edgar was too busy. He was also a fine sailor. In winter he stored his sailboat in their carriage house. (After a lengthy search, the aunts had found a toy sailboat and stored it in the carriage house of the dollhouse.)

"You grow younger every day," he told them.

"Tush," they said, but beamed as they took his coat and scarf.

"Any leaks or squeaks to report?"

"Not today," Judith said. "Today is a day of rest."

"For everyone but you two," Adam grinned.

"Oh—we do have one problem," Emily murmured, and told him about the mice.

"No problem, I'll take care of it," he promised and moved into the parlor.

The doorbell.

"Pamela," the aunts said in unison.

Pamela was always late. The eldest niece, she was a dedicated career woman with a Ph.D. in psychology and her work was so important and her time—so valuable. They opened the door to find her poised on the top step, trim and erect, with an almost military bearing.

"Hello, Aunts," she said gruffly, giving them each a quick peck on the cheek. "Sorry I'm late," she added, not sounding a bit sorry. She handed her coat to Emily, her stylish paisley shawl to Judith, and glanced toward the parlor. "I see the clan has gathered."

"Yes, dear. They're all in there," Emily said.

"Go in and warm yourself with some sherry," Judith urged.

The voices of "the clan" blurred into an indistinguishable din as the cut-glass sherry decanter was emptied. The aunts did not believe in hors d'oeuvres on Thanksgiving. "It's a sin to spoil their appetites before a big dinner," they reasoned.

After about half an hour, Emily came to the parlor door with a little brass bell. She had to ring it several times before the guests relinquished their glasses and made their way into the dining room.

CHAPTER 2

As usual, the dinner was a great success. The company were on their best behavior (for the aunts' sakes). Despite differences between some family members, they all shared a mutual fondness for the aunts.

Judith sat at the foot of the table, near the kitchen, so she could move in and out easily with the food. Emily sat next to her, serving the vegetables. Edgar occupied the head of the table and was in charge of the carving. Ranged along one side was the Turner family; Susanne, Adam, Amanda, and Tad. Across from them were the Pancoasts; Tom, Mildred, Molly, and Tommy Junior. Perched at the end of these rows, facing each other, were Marie and Pamela. The baby was ensconced in an old-fashioned cane highchair, which would have failed all modern safety standards.

When Mildred launched into a long diatribe about how astrology (her passion) should be included "right up there with the rest of the sciences," Adam, the physics teacher, held his tongue. His only sign of agitation was the way he repeatedly aligned his silverware and water goblet. And when Tom stated that "the crime rate would go down if women would just stay home and look after their kids," Pamela gritted her teeth but remained mum.

"Which one shot the turkey this year?" Edgar teased his older sisters playfully. "The aunts share all the domestic chores, you know." He winked at the others. "I was wondering which one was the best shot?"

"Now, Edgar," Judith said, "you know perfectly well we always buy our turkey from Mr. Beesley, the butcher."

"Of course. But one year, I think you should run into the woods and take a shot at one—like our Pilgrim fathers used to do. It would be more economical—"

The picture of either roly-poly Judith or pencil-thin Emily running through the woods with a shotgun made everybody laugh.

"To begin with," said Emily, ignoring the laughter, "our forefathers weren't Pilgrims, they were whalers, and they probably ate whale meat on Thanksgiving. They never stayed on land long enough to go traipsing after turkeys."

"Did they wish on a whale bone instead of a wishbone, Aunt Emily?" asked Amanda, the brightest child.

More laughter.

"I don't know, dear, but I know one thing—they used whale oil to light their lamps."

"Can we go see the whale after dinner?" begged Tad. He was referring to the skeleton of a whale housed in the Seacrest Marine Museum. Other items on display were scrimshaw carved from whale bones and tusks by sailors (between whales), bits of masts and sails, and even some old Spanish coins cast up from shipwrecks long ago. Today, after a bad storm, coins were still occasionally found on the beach at Seacrest. The Pancoasts had quite a collection of them stashed away in the attic.

"I'm sorry, dear," Emily said. "The museum is closed on Thanksgiving."

"We can play hide-and-seek," Susanne said quickly, to soften her son's disappointment.

"Are these vegetables from your garden, Judith?" asked Marie, changing the subject.

"Yes, the cabbage in the coleslaw, the onions, and the sweet potatoes all came from our garden," Judith said proudly.

Everyone praised their fresh flavor.

And so the meal progressed through turkey, stuffing, vegetables, cranberry sauce, and gravy—to the pumpkin pie. (There was ice cream molded into shapes of pumpkins and turkeys for the children.) The children finished first and were excused to go play, but the adults lingered over their dessert and coffee. When they were about to push back their chairs, Amanda came running in. She ran straight up to her mother and whispered urgently in her ear.

"Amanda, it's not polite to—" Susanne began, but stopped. "Show me." She rose quickly and followed her daughter out of the room.

A minute later, Adam rose and joined them.

Those remaining at the table heard voices rising in the hall.

"Who could have done it?"

"It must have been one of the children."

"Oh no, they love the dollhouse."

"I'll go round them up."

By then everyone had gathered in the hall and was staring at the dollhouse. The small dining room was topsy-turvy: chairs overturned, silverware scattered, napkins and goblets on the floor. And one of the dolls, the one fashioned to resemble Pamela, was slumped over, face down in her plate.

"It wasn't the children," Emily said gravely.

"Who was it then?" asked Marie.

"Mice," said Judith quickly. "Adam's going to take care of them for us, aren't you, Adam?"

"Right," Adam nodded.

"Let's all go into the parlor and have some fun." Edgar led the way.

The others followed. All except Judith and Emily, who lingered in the hall.

"Twice in one day?" Judith whispered.

"And in the *same* room." Emily shook her head.

When the two aunts reentered the parlor they each wore a fixed smile for the company.

Mildred was beginning a jigsaw puzzle. The kind of mindless activity that Marie, a creative artist, could never understand. Pamela had started working the *Times* crossword puzzle. She claimed she could complete any crossword puzzle in less than an hour, barring interruptions. (Mildred had always wanted to test her claim by locking her up alone in a room without a dictionary.) Edgar gamely began trying to drum up some interest in charades. Adam was sitting by the window, watching the older children playing tag on the front lawn. Tom eyed the clock, waiting for the right moment to duck out to the Seacrest Inn for a drink. As the aunts approached Susanne, she launched into an anecdote about her son, Tad.

"On Halloween he went trick-or-treating dressed as a bear and someone gave him a jar of honey. At which point," Susanne related, "he tore off his mask and said hotly, 'I'm not a real bear and I'd rather have a candy bar, please.'"

The aunts laughed.

"Anybody for charades?" Edgar persisted.

Groans from various parts of the room.

"I'm off for a breath of fresh air," Tom said, heading for the front door.

"There," Mildred said, placing a piece in her puzzle.

"Does anyone know a word for 'procure'?" Pamela asked.

"Get," said Adam.

". . . with six letters?"

"Obtain?" suggested Emily, hesitantly.

"Right, Aunt. Thanks."

Edgar finally succeeded in recruiting a small group—the aunts, Susanne, and himself—to play charades. Adam, tired of rearranging the knickknacks on the coffee table, excused himself with, "Think I'll go set those mousetraps." Mildred retreated to a corner with her cellular phone to check in with her astrologist. The baby was napping. And Pamela, distracted by the "ungodly noise" made by the charaders, announced she was taking her crossword into the dining room, "where I can cogitate in peace."

· · ·

It was almost dark when the first guests began to make noises about going home. Tom had arrived back from his "breath of fresh air," singing a college song and smelling strongly of whiskey. Mildred began quickly packing up the baby's things and ordering the older children to get their coats. Taking their cue from her, the Turners began searching for their children's belongings. A hunt for a stray mitten took Susanne into the dining room. The rest of the party was startled by her piercing cry.

The room was in total disarray. Chairs overturned, contents of goblets and coffee cups spilled, napkins scattered. And slumped at the table, facedown in her dessert plate, was Pamela.

CHAPTER 3

When the phone rang, Dr. Fenimore was alone in his office. Mrs. Doyle—his nurse, secretary, office manager, and chief bottle washer—had gone out on an errand. He picked up the receiver.

"Oh, I'm sorry to bother you, Doctor—"

Emily Pancoast. She and her sister had been patients of his for years, and his father's before him.

"No bother," he said. "What can I do for you, Miss Pancoast?"

"I wouldn't have called the office, but it's about my niece, Pamela. You may have seen—"

He vaguely remembered seeing an obituary for a Pamela Pancoast recently and wondered if there was a connection. (Reading the obit column was part of Fenimore's job. Both his jobs.) "Oh . . . ah . . . yes. Terrible tragedy. So young. I should have writ—"

"Oh no. We wouldn't expect . . . I mean, that's not why I called."

"Oh?"

"I called to consult you in your other capacity, as . . . er—" She faltered.

Dr. Fenimore tried to keep his two occupations separate, but sometimes they inevitably overlapped. "As an investigator?" He helped her out.

"Yes, that's it." Emily sighed with relief. "You see, Doctor, just before Pamela died, there was a disturbance in the doll-house and Pamela's doll was . . . "

Fenimore was familiar with the Pancoasts' famous dollhouse and the dolls which represented each member of the family. "Go on," he prompted.

"Doctor, Pamela's doll died—in a similar manner to Pamela."

When Mrs. Doyle came back from her errand, she found her employer preoccupied. She had to speak to him twice before he answered, and then his answer was unsatisfactory.

"What? Oh, you're back," he said.

"I asked if you wanted me to order more flu vaccine. We're almost out."

"Hmm."

"Is that a 'yes'?"

"Oh yes. Sure. Go ahead."

"How much?"

"How much what?"

"Vaccine."

He shrugged. "Oh, another dozen shots."

She made a note and turned back to her typewriter. He had offered to buy her a word processor, but she had refused. None of those newfangled dinguses for her. That was one of the reasons she and the doctor got on so well. They both hated change and liked to preserve the old. He maintained a solo practice when every other doctor had joined a group or an HMO. And he still made house calls. He never pressured her to learn new procedures or operate new equipment, as long as she produced her work on time.

The office occupied the front half of the first floor of his old town house on Spruce Street and he had not changed anything in it since his father died twenty years ago. It was a hodgepodge of hand-me-down furniture and knickknacks picked up at thrift shops and the Salvation Army. His father's 1890s microscope still sat on his desk under a bell jar (which Mrs. Doyle dusted religiously) and the creaky centrifuge his father had used for spinning down urine samples still rested on a windowsill. Fenimore used it occasionally. "Why not, if it works?" he argued.

"I had a call while you were out," he said abruptly.

"Oh?"

"Emily Pancoast."

"Not her heart, I hope." Emily had had a pacemaker installed several years ago.

"No. Her niece just died." And he told her about the doll.

"Couldn't she have been mistaken? I mean, maybe it just fell over, or one of the children—"

"It happened twice. The first time they blamed it on a mouse. Then it happened again—in the same room."

" 'The *Two* Bad Mice,' " said Mrs. Doyle.

"In the *same* room, Doyle." He glared at her.

His glare didn't bother her. She was too excited. He only called her "Doyle" when they were about to embark on a case.

Mrs. Doyle called up a picture of Emily, the elder Pancoast sister—her straight back and stern mouth (which broke into a surprising smile at the slightest hint of a joke). She would never disturb Dr. Fenimore on a mere whim. She must sincerely suspect something—or someone. She was thoughtful as she returned to her typing, part of her mind remaining with the dollhouse. She had never seen it herself, but the doctor had described it in detail to her many times. It was the prize of Seacrest. Everyone who summered there knew about it. And every Christmas the sisters held an open house for the local people to come view it. They couldn't have an open house in the summer because the crowds would have been too great.

"What's my schedule tomorrow, Doyle?"

Pulling back from her reverie, she checked his calendar. "Three patients in the morning—"

"And the afternoon?"

"Only one. Mr. Elkton at three o'clock."

"Could you move him up to noon?"

"I suppose—"

"Think I'll nip down to Seacrest tomorrow. The funeral's at four."

The door to the cellar flew open. Doctor and nurse turned

abruptly. A Hispanic teenager emerged with a smudge of dirt under one eye and a cobweb over one ear.

"When did you last clean that place?" Horatio glared at his employer.

"Why, uh—" Fenimore stuttered.

Mrs. Doyle's eye was drawn to the rolled-up paper tube under the boy's arm. "What's that?" she demanded. She always suspected Horatio of light-fingered tendencies. (The name "Horatio" was a gift from his mother when she ran out of saints. Her nickname for him was "Ray," but he preferred to be called "Rat.")

"Just some old poster," the boy muttered.

"Let me see."

Reluctantly Horatio unrolled the tube, revealing a replica of a famous painting. In the warm sepia tones popular at the turn of the century, a dramatic scene was depicted. A small child lay outstretched on a makeshift bed. From one end of the room, her father stared at her anxiously. At a table nearby, her mother sat, head bent in distress. To the left of the child was a neatly groomed man with a beard. He too stared at the child. But his expression was more thoughtful than anxious. The caption under the painting read: "The Doctor."

"I love that picture," Mrs. Doyle sighed. "You'll never see the likes of him again."

Fenimore looked slightly put out.

"What d'ya mean?" asked Horatio.

"He's kind and good and—not rich," she said.

"Can't you be kind and good *and* rich?" the boy countered.

18

"It's *much* harder," Mrs. Doyle said firmly and turned back to her typewriter.

"Let me see, Rat." Fenimore reached for the poster. Glancing at the bottom, he read the inscription aloud: "Keep politics out of this picture." His laugh was harsh. " 'Keep *profit* out of this picture' is more like it." He handed it back to the boy.

"Can I keep it?"

"It's an antique," Mrs. Doyle objected.

"Why do you want it?" Fenimore was curious.

"It's a nice picture. We don't have any. My mom'd like it."

"Help yourself," Fenimore shrugged. "It's a dead issue," he added, more to himself than to them.

Bewildered by the reaction caused by his new acquisition, Horatio rolled it up and carefully slipped a rubber band around it. He turned back to his employer. "When did you last clean out that cellar?" he repeated. "It's a fuckin' fire hazard."

Mrs. Doyle winced. She had hoped after a year in the doctor's employ, the boy's language would have improved.

Fenimore looked guilty.

"You could have a great yard sale!" The boy brightened. "I'll help you clean it out, if you give me a cut."

Such business enterprise in one so young impressed Fenimore. "Well, now—"

"Just a minute," said Mrs. Doyle. "If there are to be any cuts around here, I want—"

"Enough!" Fenimore held up his hands. "I have more important things to think about than cellars and yard sales. We can discuss this later. Back to work."

Grumbling, his employees obeyed, and Fenimore placed a long distance telephone call.

"The Seacrest Police Department, please."

Mrs. Doyle paused in her typing to blatantly eavesdrop.

"This is Dr. Fenimore, the Pancoasts' family physician. I've just learned about the death of Pamela Pancoast—"

A long silence followed during which Fenimore listened intently. "Is that so? Interesting. I'll drop by tomorrow. Around two?"

When he replaced the receiver, Mrs. Doyle noticed a change in her employer's expression. From grave anxiety to eager anticipation.

CHAPTER 4

As Fenimore charged up to the front door of the Henderson Funeral Home, a carefully coifed young man in a dark suit was withdrawing his key from the lock.

"I'm sorry, sir." He bestowed a grave smile on Fenimore (the one they practiced to perfection in mortuary school). "The Pancoast family has just left. But they are receiving up at the house, if you wish to pay your respects."

Fenimore glanced at the program the young man handed him. At the top, in elegant script, was written:

In Loving Memory of Pamela Pancoast

And at the bottom, in italics:

The family welcomes friends at home
immediately after the ceremony

"Thanks." Fenimore folded the sheet into four unequal parts and stuffed it into his side jacket pocket (which was already overflowing with a syringe in a plastic wrapper, several bottles of pills, and his stethoscope).

He strolled back to his car. No rush now. His lengthy but informative visit with the coroner had caused him to miss the funeral, and the reception would probably go on for hours. There would be no opportunity to have a word with the family members alone for some time. And he certainly could not impart his newfound knowledge about Pamela's death to a crowd of gawking mourners.

Fenimore cruised idly down the main street of Seacrest. There is nothing more depressing than a seaside resort in November. The storefronts were as bleak and shorn as an actress after removing her makeup and wig. And the display windows were as empty and forlorn as the rooms of a house after moving day. The only store that showed any signs of life was an inconspicuous cinder-block structure called Ben's Variety Store. It bore a hand-painted sign: OPEN ALL YEAR. Ben's sold a little of everything—from bread and milk to nuts and bolts—to help the handful of year-round residents make it through the winter. As Fenimore drove by, he caught a glimpse of Ben puttering around inside.

At the end of the street, towering majestically above the town, was the Pancoast mansion. Built in the mid-1800s by Caleb Pancoast III, the grandfather of the present owners, it was a massive wooden edifice, dwarfing the more modest clapboard houses in the vicinity. On former visits, the Misses Pancoast had filled Fenimore in on their family history.

The original Caleb Pancoast had arrived at Seacrest from England in 1762 and set up a whaling station. The Pancoast men had been great whalers. And the Pancoast women had been great "waiters." Pacing the widow's walk that was attached to the sea side of the house, they had anxiously watched and waited for the return of their seamen from their long voyages. When the whaling industry died out, the Pancoasts switched to fishing and shipbuilding. And when that was no longer lucrative, they had become simply—builders. In recent years, they had concentrated on restoring the older homes in South Jersey, of which there were many.

Today, the front door of the Pancoast house was decorated with a simple wreath of white daisies. Before ringing the bell, Fenimore tried the knob. It turned easily. The hall was crowded with people talking in subdued tones. His eyes swept over them, searching for Emily or Judith. He spied Emily near the dollhouse and moved toward her. Not an easy process. Keeping his eye fixed on the top of her head, he edged himself sideways through the crowd.

Emily glanced his way and with a glad expression began to thread her way toward him. Despite her age and frailty, she made better progress than he. "Doctor—" She took his hand. "How kind of you to come—and so promptly."

"Sorry I missed the ceremony," he muttered.

"Oh, Doctor." Judith came up behind him. "How nice of you to make the trip. Do have some coffee or tea. It's in there." She pointed to the overflowing dining room. And both older ladies were carried away from him on the tide of their guests.

Rather than fight his way to the refreshments, Fenimore

decided to take a look at the dollhouse—the focal point of the vast hall. It stood at the bottom of the staircase on a platform which had been erected expressly for its display. Several other people were discreetly examining it also. For an instant Fenimore thought there was a miniature funeral wreath fastened to the small front door—identical to the one on the door of the big house. (He was familiar with the eccentricities of the Pancoast sisters where their elaborate toy was concerned.) But on closer examination, he was relieved to find a cluster of Indian corn. As he inspected the exquisitely furnished rooms, he recalled what he knew about the house.

Edgar Pancoast, the aunts' younger brother, had surprised his sisters one Christmas with the dollhouse. Although chief architect of the family firm, it had taken him a year—applying all his building acumen—to complete it. There was no doubt it was an amazing structure. It had the two chimneys, gabled roofs, and rambling screen porch of the big house, and was decorated with the same delicate squiggles and scrolls of gingerbread. Edgar had even included the carriage house (now converted to a garage) with its cupola and delicate wrought-iron weather vane. (He had spent a long, hot afternoon plying the local blacksmith with beer to get him to produce that!) The plumbing fixtures and electricity had been supplied by Adam, his son-in-law. But the interior he had left to his sisters. It had been up to them to paper and paint and furnish it. This they had done with the greatest enthusiasm.

Immersing themselves in the world of miniatures, they had read everything about dollhouses they could get their hands on. They had visited the famous Queen Mary dollhouse between the World Wars and it had made a deep impression. (Secretly, Emily thought she looked a little like Queen Mary). They had especially admired the toothbrushes. One of the guidebooks said the bristles were made from "the finest hair taken from inside the ear of a goat." When they were furnishing their own dollhouse and had come to the bathroom accessories, Judith had wondered aloud what they should use for the toothbrush bristles. "There are no goats in Seacrest," Emily said, emphatically, "so put that right out of your mind." Instead, they had settled for hairs snipped from the tail of a neighbor's cat.

Somehow the two sisters had managed to find a facsimile of every piece of furniture that occupied the larger house. The wickerware on the porch, the mahogany in the parlor (they still called it that), the oak in the dining room, and the bird's-eye maple in the spare bedroom. The tea set of pink English china had been acquired at the gift shop of the Victoria & Albert Museum by one of the family's travelers and the crystal chandelier had been captured by a niece at an auction at Sotheby's.

The whole family had been caught up in the project and every member had contributed by either buying or making something. Judith had written a minute book of love poems in her own hand. And Emily had painted two seascapes the size of postage stamps which were identical to the ones that hung in their real dining room. And both sisters had filled tiny buckets with sand to place in each corner of the widow's walk in case of fire—a custom they had read about in a journal of one of their ancestors. Even Dr. Fenimore had contributed. He had donated a syringe with which they had injected a fine sherry into the cut-glass decanter, and a hemostat for removing its small top. The hemostat worked like a pair of scissors, but instead of blades that came to a point, it had blunt ends like a tweezer. Both sisters had a touch of arthritis which made them clumsy and the hemostat enabled them to handle small objects more easily.

When the furnishings had been completed—down to the last picture on the wall and the last pot in the kitchen, it seems the aunts had grown restless. Surely there was something more. . . . The story went that one evening Emily had been reading a book about antique dolls. Suddenly she had looked up and said, "What about dolls, Judith?"

"Oh, Emily, you're a genius." Judith pounced on the idea. "I'll start making them tonight. One for each member of the family."

"You must let me help," Emily said. "It was my idea."

"Of course." And Judith headed for the sewing room to round up fabric, cotton batting, needles, thread, scissors, and paint—all the materials necessary to fashion miniature dolls.

Once the dolls were created, the two sisters became quite carried away with them. When their nephew, Tom, stayed with them one summer—bartending at the Seacrest Inn—he kept his red sports car parked in their carriage house. Right away, the aunts went to the dime store and bought a toy plastic car— the same shade of red as Tom's—and placed his doll in it. At night they parked the car in the dollhouse carriage house for the length of his stay. Another time, when Pamela was awarded her doctorate degree, they dressed her doll in a cap and gown, complete with velvet hood the same shade of blue as her real hood. Mildred thought the aunts overdid the doll thing. When she married Tom she refused to have a doll made in her like-ness. She wrote in her diary: "I hated to disappoint the aunts, but I don't want some doll that looks like me running around loose. It gives me the creeps. What if someone took a dislike to me and decided to stick pins in it?" But she was the only one who objected to this family tradition.

Gradually, the guests (if that's the correct designation for fu-neral attenders) began taking their leave and Fenimore was able to make his way into the dining room. Soon all that remained were himself and members of the Pancoast family. The adults, that is. The children, twelve and under, had been excluded on the pretext that exposure to death might upset them (although they were exposed to a steady diet of violent death on television every day).

Fenimore found a cup of coffee and a chair. Once seated, he sipped his coffee and settled back to wait for someone to broach the subject which had brought them all there.

CHAPTER 5

Marie, Pamela's mother, was the first to raise the subject. She drew up a chair beside Fenimore and confided, "My daughter Pamela was too young to record her burial wishes, but I did overhear her say once that she wanted to be cremated and 'tossed to the four winds.'" The cremation had been taken care of, but the contents of the small wooden box on the mantel still awaited disposal. How this was to be accomplished had yet to be decided, although several suggestions had been made.

Adam, the physics teacher, had suggested they divide the ashes into four parts, check the direction of the wind each day, i.e., north, south, east, or west, and scatter one fourth of the amount on the appropriate day. Tom had come up with another, less scientific scheme: wait for the hurricane season, toss the whole lot out at once, and trust the wind to carry the ashes off in all directions—and with much less fuss.

Fenimore was impressed by both ideas, but thought the latter had more flair.

"We do appreciate your coming. . . ." Marie murmured to Fenimore.

"When we know how busy you are . . ." Judith said.

"And such a long distance . . ." Emily added.

It was obvious that Emily had not informed the family about her phone call to the doctor. And Fenimore had not informed Emily about the other, more urgent reason which had brought him hurtling down to Seacrest.

"Nonsense," Fenimore assured them, almost adding, "Wouldn't have missed it for the world," but caught himself in time. Awful how frequently funerals took on the character of a party, he thought. But, after scanning the faces of his companions (their color and animation had increased markedly since he had arrived), he revised his opinion. A little party atmosphere was probably a good thing. The Irish Catholics had the right idea—providing plenty of whiskey at their wakes. He could use a drink himself right now. Unfortunately, the Pancoasts were Presbyterians.

"Would you like some sherry, Doctor?" Judith had read his mind.

He would have preferred Scotch, but he settled for sherry.

When everyone was supplied with refreshments, the aunts with their cups of tea and Marie and Fenimore with their thimblefuls of sherry, he began gingerly, "I wonder if you could tell me what time you discovered the . . . uh . . . deceased?"

Marie looked away in distress. Judith and Emily exchanged glances, each hoping the other would answer. Finally Judith spoke. "We had just finished a game of charades. It was beginning to grow dark. I think it was about five o'clock."

While Fenimore began his impromptu interrogation, the other family members drew near. Even Mildred, who had been huddled in a corner with her cellular phone, put it away and joined the others.

"And after you found her, what did you do then?"

Edgar tried mouth-to-mouth resus . . . oh, dear . . ." Emily could not go on.

"And I called the ambulance," Judith said.

"They came right away," Mildred put in.

"Yes, they were very quick," Susanne agreed.

"I believe," Adam said, "the preliminary cause of death was 'asphyxiation due to aspiration.' "

"He means she choked," Tom broke in, helping himself to the sherry decanter. (From somewhere he had acquired a large tumbler.)

"Was anyone present in the house besides the family?" Fenimore asked.

"No," Judith said firmly.

"There was Carrie," Emily corrected her.

"Oh yes. But she just popped in at the end."

"Carrie?"

"A child from the village. We hire her sometimes to help clean up after parties," Judith explained. "She comes from a large family and appreciates the chance to earn a little extra money."

"Did Carrie have anything to do with the food preparations?"

"Oh no. I did all that myself." Judith was unable to conceal a note of pride.

"I peeled the potatoes and onions," Emily reminded her mildly.

"In fact," Judith continued, "I sent Carrie home right after the . . . when the paramedics left. And Emily and I did the cleanup ourselves the next day."

"If dinner was over, why was Pamela in the dining room— alone?" pressed Fenimore.

"She wanted to finish her crossword puzzle 'in peace,'" Susanne explained.

Judith looked slightly embarrassed. "You see, Doctor, when we play charades, we get quite raucous."

"Pamela was always stretching her mind." Edgar quickly came to his daughter's defense. "She didn't have time for frivolity."

"Did anything else happen prior to her death, besides the two upsets in the dollhouse?"

"*Two* upsets?" Edgar repeated.

The sisters looked embarrassed.

"Yes," Judith finally answered their questioning stares. "The dining room in the dollhouse was disturbed once before you came."

"We blamed it on mice," Emily murmured.

"Why the third degree, Doc?" Tom, fortified with sherry, broke the strained silence.

(Emily and Judith were the only ones who knew about the doctor's avocation.)

Fenimore cleared his throat. "I'm afraid I'm here under false pretenses." He looked only faintly chagrined. "You see, I learned yesterday from the coroner that the autopsy report on

Pamela disagreed with the preliminary cause of death."

He had everyone's fixed attention.

"Now they believe she was poisoned."

"I knew it!" cried Mildred. "Pluto moved into the Twelth House today, and that always means disaster!" Her comment was punctuated by the doorbell's harsh clamor.

Judith started up, but Dr. Fenimore placed a restraining hand on her arm. "Let me go," he said gently. "That will be the police."

CHAPTER 6

When the police had finished their questioning and left with their standard warning, "No one is to leave the area until this matter is cleared up," Fenimore set about restoring the family's equilibrium.

"It's not enough to lose your daughter," Edgar fumed, "but you also have to put up with the police."

"Don't, dear." Marie squeezed his hand.

"It's just routine, sir," Fenimore soothed. "Until the real culprit is found."

"I think it's dreadful," Emily said. "Why, it was probably a simple case of food poisoning."

"I'm sure everything I cooked was fresh, Emily," Judith turned on her sister.

"Oh. I didn't mean—" Emily bit her tongue.

"Have they determined what poison was used?" Adam asked.

Fenimore nodded. "But I'm not at liberty to divulge—"

"Say—exactly what do *you* have to do with all this, anyway?"

Tom demanded. "Are you somekindofa private dick or something?"

Fenimore coughed. "Let's say I'm a family friend with experience in criminal investigations and a knowledge of police procedures. I thought I might be useful to you, but if you would prefer . . ."

"Oh no, Doctor." Judith was aghast. "Please stay."

"Yes. We're so grateful." Emily cast Tom a withering look.

The others nodded in agreement. Tom left the room in a sulk.

"Perhaps she had some jealous colleague in the academic world who wanted to do her in," suggested Adam. A member of the academic community himself, he knew the power of such emotions.

"So Professor what's-his-name crept in the back door with a spoonful of cyanide, carried it into the dining room where Pamela just happened to be, and said, 'Here, dearie, have a taste,' and left the same way." Mildred's voice had a hysterical edge.

"What about the dollhouse?" Marie reminded them. "Only a member of the family would think of disturbing that."

Avoiding one another's eyes, they silently pondered her words.

"Anyone for a drink?" Tom stood in the doorway waving a bottle of brandy.

"Oh, Tom, you've been into the medicine cabinet!" Judith cried.

"I think we could all use a little medicine tonight." He

34

splashed a large dose of the brown liquid into the tumbler that had recently held his sherry.

"Tom, I want to go home," Mildred pleaded. "I promised the sitter we'd be home hours ago."

"That's my wife for you. She's suspected of murder and worries about the sitter!" He wasn't about to give up his hard-won prize so easily.

"I think we should all go home," Fenimore said quickly, "and give the aunts a rest." For a moment his detective self gave way to his physician self; he had noticed that the two elderly women looked worn-out.

Everyone looked at the aunts and came to the same conclusion. Susanne and Adam started to move to the coat closet. The rest followed. Even Tom gulped his drink and accepted his coat from his wife.

Fenimore was the last to leave. "Could you give me Carrie's address? I'd like to drop by and have a word with her."

Judith gave him her address and the directions to her house.

"If it's agreeable," he said, "I'd like to do some unofficial snooping."

"Oh, Doctor, thank you," Emily said.

"We didn't dare hope . . ." Judith's voice overflowed with gratitude. She knew the doctor only accepted the cases of very special friends.

"I'll be in touch." He set off on foot in search of Carrie, whistling. Suddenly remembering the somber nature of the occasion, Fenimore stopped. But as soon as he was out of earshot, he took it up again even more vigorously.

CHAPTER 7

Carrie lived in a small cottage tucked behind the inn, on the wrong side of town. Fenimore decided to walk. He could always think better on foot. Carrie was sixteen, the oldest child in a family of six, Judith had told him. She served as a surrogate mother to her younger brothers and sisters because her mother was an alcoholic. Her father had left them years ago.

The house was a summer bungalow that someone had attempted, ineffectively, to winterize. Dirty sheets of plastic were tacked across the windows on the sea side of the house and tufts of pink insulation stuck out between the windows and their wooden frames. Tacked to the front door was a handwritten note: "Bell don't work. Knock loud." When Fenimore knocked, a teenage girl answered the door. Two towheaded youngsters clung to her legs and an odor of cabbage and cats overwhelmed him.

"Are you Carrie?"

She nodded.

She looked tired and older than her years. He was sorry he had come without warning. He hastened to make amends. "Sorry to burst in on you like this. I'm Dr. Fenimore, a friend of the Pancoasts. I hear you were helping out there on Thanksgiving Day, when the unfortunate . . . er . . . accident occurred."

"Oh yes. I came to wash up." Two more towheads, of varying sizes, appeared behind their sister to stare owl-like at Fenimore.

"I wonder if we might talk?"

"Sure." She shook herself free of the children. "Scat, now."

They scattered like leaves to the four corners, but remained in the room. She led him to a decrepit couch in front of a cold fireplace. A pair of rusted andirons stood inside, but there were no logs in sight. Carrie unceremoniously dismissed a limp gray cat from the seat of a wooden rocker. The chair had obviously seen heavy use—one arm was missing and the brown paint was worn and chipped. A TV droned with a soap opera in another part of the house.

"There was something funny about Miss Pamela's death, wasn't there?" Carrie took her seat in the rocker. "She didn't choke like they said, did she?"

Modern telecommunications were no match for the village grapevine, Fenimore decided. "That's right," he said.

She waited expectantly for more information, but none was forthcoming.

"What time did you arrive at the Pancoasts'?"

She frowned. "It was getting dark. It must have been nearly five. I told Miss Judith I couldn't come earlier because I had my own family to feed."

"Of course. When you arrived, what was the first thing you did?"

"Well, I came in the back door—they always leave it open. The kitchen was a terrible mess. Pots and pans all over the place. Miss Judith is a wonderful cook, but sloppy!" She raised her eyebrows. "Then I decided to check the dining room and see if the table had been cleared. Of course it wasn't. The dessert dishes were still there. But things were even worse than usual. Chairs were turned upside down, dishes were on the floor. I remember thinking, it must have been some party!"

Fenimore waited.

"And then I noticed Miss Pamela—her head was on the table. At first I thought she had fallen asleep or passed out. Sometimes folks take a bit too much on the holidays," she confided knowingly.

Fenimore nodded encouragingly. "What did you do next?"

"Well, I was trying to decide whether to wake her. She's a bit of a crank at the best of times—" She placed a hand over her mouth, remembering she was speaking of the dead.

Fenimore smiled. "Go on."

"I decided she'd take my head off if I woke her, so I quietly cleared the plates around her and went back to the kitchen."

"And then?"

"I hadn't been there more than a minute when I heard someone scream. Then there was all this commotion. There's a little window in the top of the kitchen door. I peeked through that and saw Mr. Edgar shaking his daughter. Then he dragged her down on the floor and started breathing mouth to mouth. Miss

Judith almost knocked me over when she burst into the kitchen. She wanted to use the phone in the pantry to call the ambulance."

"What did you do then?"

She shrugged. "I started to clean up the kitchen."

"In spite of all the commotion?"

"Oh yes. You see, I'm used to commotion." She nodded at the towheads around the room. Two had crept over to her while she was talking. One hung on the back of her chair. The other knelt beside her, his head in her lap. She had been stroking his hair absently as she talked. "Not a week goes by that we don't call the Emergency because one of them's fallen out of a tree or swallowed a button or something." When Carrie smiled, her face lost its careworn expression and Fenimore was reminded how young she was.

"I see." He smiled. "You do have your hands full." He glanced around the room. "I'm sorry to have taken so much of your time." He stood up.

"No trouble." She gently removed her brother's head from her lap and rose too. "Wouldn't you like a cup of tea?" Belatedly, she remembered her manners.

"No thanks. I have to get back to Philadelphia."

From Carrie's expression, he might have been returning to Mars.

He shook her hand. "You've been very helpful." As he started out the door, he turned. "No one else came into the kitchen while you were there?"

"No, sir. Except Miss Judith—to tell me to go home. Before

39

I'd half finished the cleanup too. And the next day she came here to pay me my money. The full amount, although I told her it wasn't right."

He thanked Carrie again and left her as he had found her, standing in the doorway, two children clinging to her. Confound it, where was the child's mother? It wasn't right shoving all that responsibility on a teenager. She should be at her studies. Or with friends—having a good time. Absorbed in his anger, he almost forgot where he was going. Then he saw the lighted sign. SEACREST INN. It had grown dark while he was talking to Carrie. And colder. A sea breeze in November was no joke. Pulling his coat more closely about him, he headed for the glowing sign.

CHAPTER 8

The bar wasn't crowded. But there were more people than Fenimore would have expected on an off-season evening. The decor was "fake seacoast." Garish reproductions of sailing ships alternated with fishnets and lobster pots along the walls. A large ship's wheel hung behind the bar. Anchors decorated every available surface—napkins, glasses, ashtrays, and coasters. Fenimore supposed that the captain's cap that the bartender wore at such a rakish angle had once been white. He ordered Scotch.

At the other end of the bar a small group of locals were discussing something in subdued tones. Fenimore could barely hear them, but every now and then a voice would rise and he caught the name "Pancoast." He knew the family had founded the village of Seacrest before the American Revolution. There was a Pancoast Street and a Pancoast Library. Any happening in the Pancoast family—birth, wedding, death—would be of major interest to the inhabitants of the village. If the group at the end of the bar had access to the same grapevine as Carrie—there could be no doubt about what topic they were discussing.

Gradually Fenimore began to grow warmer. He shed his coat, folded it, and placed it on the barstool next to him.

"Remember old Caleb Pancoast?" A voice rumbled down the bar. "There was a seaman for you." The voice went on to relate a sea story of which Fenimore caught only snatches.

"Eighty-mile-an-hour winds . . ."

"Torn sail . . ."

"Busted rudder . . ."

Now and then the men would send wary glances down the bar and lower their voices. A stranger in a small town was always suspect.

Fenimore kept his eyes focused on himself in the mirror behind the bar (something he rarely did; he did not consider his face one of his fine points). He ordered another Scotch. When the bartender set it down, Fenimore asked, "Do the Pancoasts ever come in here?"

The bartender pushed back his cap and grinned. "Sure, Doc. Miss Judith and Miss Emily come waltzing in here every afternoon for a snort."

Fenimore wasn't surprised that the man knew he was a doctor. Just another example of the village grapevine at work. He laughed. "I meant the younger generation."

"Only Tom. He's a booze hound."

Fenimore didn't contradict him.

"But then, you can hardly blame him—with that wife of his. Doesn't make a move without reading her horoscope first. Uses a cell phone to check in with her astrologer twenty-four hours a day. Spends as much money on fortune-tellers as most women spend on hairdressers." He took a swipe at the bar with his cloth. "A real nut. If she were mine, I'd drink too. As a matter of fact, Tom was in here on Thanksgiving."

"You were open Thanksgiving?"

"Oh, yeah. Hafta keep the dining room open for the lazy broads who don't want to cook—or have forgotten how. Of course we're open."

"Yo, Frank!" Someone signaled for his services at the other end of the bar.

Fenimore put down a generous tip and started to leave. When the first blast of cold air hit him, he remembered his coat and turned back. As he reentered the bar, he was met with raucous laughter. It stopped when they saw him.

"Hey, mister!" The loudest member of the group sidled up to him. He wasn't a tall man, but he was solidly built. When he was face to face with Fenimore, he said, "You a friend of the Pancoasts?"

Fenimore nodded.

The man shared a wink with his friends and turned back to him. "Maybe you can help us settle something." He thrust his face nearer.

Fenimore waited. He wasn't interested in a barroom brawl. Not that he couldn't handle it, but he had more important things to do.

"We have a wager going here. Some of us think the Pancoast girl died natural. Others don't. What's your opinion?"

"What makes you think I have one?"

His eyes narrowed. "The Pancoast place was swarming with police tonight. Now, that ain't natural." He was so close Fenimore could smell the beer and peanuts on his breath. "You was up there, weren't you?"

It was as if the fella were accusing *him* of Pamela's death. But Fenimore understood. The man was proud of the Pancoast family, as were most of the villagers. If there was something fishy going on, he would rather blame an outsider than a member of the family—or the town.

He hesitated. But, he told himself, you can never hide the truth for long. And certainly not in a village of three hundred odd. It would probably be in all the newspapers tomorrow. He looked the man straight in the eye and said, "She may have been poisoned."

The man's belligerence evaporated. He wilted like a sail that's been suddenly lowered.

His friends had heard Fenimore too. "I told ya, Louie," one of them yelled. "You owe me a fiver."

Fenimore took his coat from the bar stool and left them to settle their wager.

A freezing rain had begun to fall. The street was slick and deserted. Fenimore regretted not bringing his car. As he moved up the street, he remembered how it looked in summer, overflowing with vacationers—browsing in the shops, balancing ice cream cones, and oozing with suntan lotion. He quickened his steps.

The Pancoast house was dark except for one light on the second floor. Probably the bathroom. The shade was drawn.

He was glad the aunts had taken his advice and retired early. As Fenimore watched, a distinct shadow moved across the yellow window shade. It passed quickly, but not before he noticed that the silhouette was not Judith's—with her fuzzy head of curls. And not Emily's—with her neat bun at the back of the neck. The silhouette was smooth—like an egg. Or a bald man. Fenimore hesitated before getting into his car. Should he wake the aunts and ask who was using their bathroom? There must be some simple explanation. Edgar or Tom? (Both father and son were balding.) One of them had probably dropped back after Fenimore had left and decided to spend the night. When he glanced at the window again, the light was out. All was dark and serene. Even the rain had stopped. Fenimore turned on the ignition and began the long trip back to Philadelphia.

CHAPTER 9

It's a disgrace!"

Fenimore recognized the note of righteous indignation in his nurse's voice and was instantly on guard. "What's a disgrace?"

"Those poor, defenseless, little old ladies. There aren't enough police to take care of them. They stand out there waiting for the buses to take them to church or to market—sitting ducks for muggers. 'Pow!' Some hood comes up behind them, socks them on the head with a baseball bat, grabs their pocketbook, and runs. Well, I'm sick of it. And I'm tired of talking about it. I'm going to do something about it!"

"What do you have in mind?" Fenimore asked cautiously.

"Karate." Mrs. Doyle had become proficient in the martial arts while serving a stint in the Navy years ago.

"For little old ladies?"

"Certainly. You just have to get them in shape. Teach 'em the techniques. They'll be a match for anyone. They have plenty of guts, but no training. Now, here's my plan. I'm going to hold classes for about twenty-five, three nights a week. When I have one class trained, they can branch out and train other groups. You know—the pyramid effect. Pretty soon we'll have a network—enough to cover the whole city. I've even thought of a name for my organization." She was so caught up with her idea, she didn't notice that Fenimore had returned to reading his mail. "The 'Red Umbrella Brigade.' Or—RUB, for short," she finished.

"Umbrellas?" His interest was rekindled by the idiocy of it. "You're going to defend yourselves against guns and knives and baseball bats—with umbrellas?"

"Of course not. The umbrella is just a symbol. When each member of the class graduates, besides a diploma, she will be awarded a red umbrella. And whenever she goes out—rain or shine—she'll carry it with her. As the reputaion of RUB grows, the hoods will learn soon enough to steer clear of my graduates—or anyone carrying a red umbrella."

"Sort of a 'Red Badge of Courage,' eh?" He was half impressed. "Where are you going to hold these classes?" He knew Mrs. Doyle had only a small apartment.

"Well, while you were in Seacrest, I went down into your cellar to see about the yard sale. And what a vast space you have down there, Doctor, once it's all cleaned out. It's a pity to let it go to waste. It would be just right for a class of about twenty-five."

"Mrs. Doyle!"

"Yes, Doctor?"

"You plan to use my cellar as a karate training ground for a bunch of octogenarians?"

"Well . . ."

"No."

"No?"

He went back to his mail.

Mrs. Doyle slid a pink message slip under his nose.

Call Mrs. Dunwoody (235-0539)
(Mugged at bus stop, 9 A.M.)

"When did this come?"

"Just a few minutes ago."

"Why didn't you tell me?" He reached for the phone.

"It's not an emergency. She's just bruised and sore." Mrs. Doyle's expression was grim.

He dialed the Dunwoody number.

"I hear you had an unfortunate accident—"

"Euphemisms," sniffed his nurse.

"How are you feeling?" Pause. "I'll be right over. Now don't leave your bed till I get there." He hung up and began organizing the contents of his briefcase. (He had been forced to abandon his cherished doctor's bag some years ago: too obvious a target for drugs.)

"Uh . . . about your cellar, Doctor—?" Mrs. Doyle handed him the otoscope he was searching for.

He tucked it into his overflowing briefcase. As he zipped the briefcase shut, he said, "If you and Horatio can empty the cellar, the ladies are welcome to it. Just see that they're out by midnight," he added tersely.

CHAPTER 10

DECEMBER

D r. Fenimore always gave his full attention to whatever he was doing at the moment. While treating Mrs. Dunwoody's cuts and bruises, the Pancoasts were far from his mind. But as soon as he was satisfied that he had done all he could for his patient, his mind returned to Seacrest.

His two interviews—one with Carrie and one with Frank, the bartender—had not furthered his investigation very much. But he had learned some things: first—that the back door to the Pancoasts' kitchen was always left open. Therefore, anyone could have gone out the front door and come in again the back way on Thanksgiving Day without being noticed. Second— Mildred Pancoast's passion for the occult was sometimes a cause of friction in the family.

When Fenimore arrived back at the office, the day's mail lay waiting on his desk. Mrs. Doyle had placed the most important piece on top—a postcard from Jennifer. Jennifer Nicholson was Fenimore's constant companion—when she was in town. Now, unfortunately, she was in the South of France. Her father, the owner and operator of an antiquarian bookstore, had sent her abroad on a search for rare books. Unlike some business trips, this one was a legitimate expense and Jennifer was expected to spend her time in metropolitan bookstores, not on Mediterranean beaches.

The back of the postcard read: "Having a lousy time. Glad you're not here." The front bore a picture of a teeming bus terminal in Marseilles.

Jennifer would have liked to be more than Fenimore's companion. But Fenimore felt diffident about their ages. She was barely twenty-five and he was pushing forty-five. Whenever he was tempted to make their relationship more permanent, he envisioned himself as a senile invalid being waited on by Jennifer in her prime, and he resisted temptation.

Before Jennifer left, she had given him a copy of her itinerary and said lightly, "Feel free to write." Fenimore had not intended to. Unlike Jennifer, he was not much of a writer. But, somehow, after she had been gone less than a week, things kept coming up that he had been used to sharing with her. He missed talking to her. To his surprise, he found himself writing to her frequently. Not short notes, but letters—often four or five pages long.

He felt like writing one now. His patient load was light this afternoon. He had a half hour before the first one was due. He cast a furtive glance at Mrs. Doyle. Assuring himself that she was immersed in Medicare forms, he slipped a piece of personal stationery out from under his blotter and began to write:

Dear Jennifer,

Upon receipt of your postcard from Marseilles this A.M, I decided to take a moment out from my heavy schedule to inform you of a recent development.

(His writing style tended toward the pedantic. On occasion, he had even been known to insert Latin phrases, such as "*tempus fugit*" or "*O tempora! O mores!*")

In this same vein, he described in detail the difficulties that had befallen the Pancoast family, filling six pages.

Now, I must draw to a close, as office hours are about to begin. But I would appreciate it if you would apply your not inconsiderable intellect to the little problem I have just described.

(Fenimore did not often indulge in flattery. This was a major departure for him.)

Sincerely, your friend,

(His signature, like his prescriptions, could have been written by a chimpanzee for all the resemblance it bore to his name.)

Checking Jennifer's itinerary, he learned that she would be in Bordeaux the following week. He placed the letter in his jacket pocket. "Think I'll get a breath of air before the next patient, Mrs. Doyle."

"Right, Doctor."

As she watched his retreating back, Mrs. Doyle wondered in which mailbox he would drop his letter to Jennifer.

When Fenimore returned, there was another phone slip on his desk. This one was marked "Urgent!" The message read, "Call Emily Pancoast re: dollhouse???" (The question marks were Mrs. Doyle's way of demanding an answer asap.)

He dialed the Pancoast number.

"Oh, Doctor. Thank you for calling back so promptly." Judith. "It's the dollhouse again. Or rather—the dolls. One of them is missing. I hate to bother you with this, and under ordinary circum—"

"Which one?"

"Tom's."

"Could you have mislaid it?"

"Oh, I don't think so. When we're here alone we always keep them in the same place—a shoe box on a shelf in the hall closet. It's so convenient to the dollhouse. I packed them up very carefully after all the . . . er . . . unpleasantness at Thanksgiving and put the box back on the shelf."

"And his doll's not in the dollhouse?"

"No. And all the rooms are in apple-pie order."

"Where is Tom now?"

"Well, that's what worries us. His wife, Mildred, called just a few minutes ago to say she was expecting him for lunch at twelve and he hadn't arrived yet. She wondered if he was here."

Fenimore checked his watch. After two.

"She said he was going to stop off here first to pick up his car. He stores it in our carriage house in bad weather and only uses it occasionally. In winter he uses their Jeep."

"Did you check the dollhouse carriage house?"

"Oh no," she said. "I didn't do that."

"Would you do it now? I'll hold."

The receiver clattered as she set it down.

"What was that all about?" Mrs. Doyle had come in to announce his next patient and caught the tail end of the conversation.

While he waited for Judith, Fenimore encapsulated the events at the Pancoast house for Mrs. Doyle.

"Doctor!" Judith was back.

"Here."

"You were right. Tom's doll *was* in the carriage house."

"And?"

"It was sitting in the little red sports car. I can't imagine who put it there. Emily swears she didn't. But I'm so relieved."

Mrs. Doyle was alarmed by the doctor's sudden pallor. "Is Edgar around?" he asked sharply.

"No. He's working on a site today."

"What about Marie?"

"She's up in her studio sculpting. She uses our attic as a studio, you know."

"Go get her and ask her to go out and check the carriage house. *Your* carriage house, not the dollhouse one." The Pancoasts had too damned many houses, he decided. "And, when you've done that, call me right back."

"I hate to interrupt Marie. . . ."

"Tell her it's an emergency. And, Judith—don't let Emily go with Marie." He had her heart condition in mind. "Call me as soon as Marie comes back."

"Yes, Doctor."

Fenimore found it hard to keep his mind on his patients— a rare situation. Fortunately, there were only a simple chest cold, a pair of swollen ankles, and a skin rash. He finished sooner than he expected. He had removed his white coat and was washing his hands when the phone rang. With a soapy hand, he snatched up the receiver.

"Is this Dr. Fenimore's office?" Not Judith. Not Emily. An official-sounding male voice.

"Speaking."

"Officer Baker here. Seacrest Police. I was told to call and give you this report."

Fenimore could have given *him* the report. "Go ahead," he said wearily.

"Friday, December second, re: Thomas Pancoast, age thirty-four. Caucasian male. Found deceased at two-thirty P.M. in his car, by his mother, Marie Pancoast, and his aunt, Judith Pancoast, the motor running." The officer's voice droned on with the details of his report. "Cause of death . . ."

"Asphyxiation by carbon monoxide," Fenimore interjected.

"That's right, sir."

Fenimore allowed the policeman to finish without further interruption.

CHAPTER 11

Because of Fenimore's previous track record for crime solving, the Seacrest Police agreed to give him a complete briefing of Tom's death.

Fenimore's next stop was the inn. The coroner had told him that there was an unusually high level of alcohol in Tom's bloodstream and Fenimore knew the inn was Tom's favorite haven for imbibing.

"Hi, Doc!" Frank hailed Fenimore as he slipped onto a barstool. "What'll it be?"

"Nothing liquid, today. I need information."

"Shoot."

"Was Tom Pancoast in here this afternoon?"

"Sure was. Left with a snootful too."

"About what time?"

Frank looked at his watch. "Came in around noon. Left about one-thirty. Plenty of time to get tanked."

"He's dead."

Frank almost dropped the glass he was polishing.

"Asphyxiated in his own car, in his aunt's carriage house."

Frank's eyes widened.

"They found him around two-thirty."

"Suicide?"

"Maybe."

"Whew!" The bartender wiped his forehead. "I knew that wife of his would get to him someday."

"Careful. That's dangerous talk."

"Right."

"Did you talk to Tom while he was here?"

"Yeah. Nothing special. Football mostly. He used to play for Brown."

Fenimore nodded. "Maybe I will take a beer. Draft."

Frank filled a glass and slid it toward him. "He didn't act depressed or nothin'," he said. "In fact, he was in a good mood. Told me a couple of jokes. This guy went into a bar—"

"Some other time, Frank."

"Oh, right." He looked sheepish.

"When he left, did he say where he was going?"

"He said he was going to 'take a ride.' The first time he said that, it scared the shit out of me, 'cause he was in no condition to drive. But then he explained—'take a ride' means he goes and sits in his car in his aunts' carriage house until he sobers up. Sometimes he even passes out there."

"Did the aunts know about this?"

"If they did, they looked the other way. They're good scouts."

"Was this habit of his—common knowledge?"

"He didn't make any secret of it." Frank ran a rag over the

56

bar. "That car was like Tom's second home. Probably wished it was his *first* home." He snapped the rag.

Fenimore finished his beer and paid for it, adding a hefty tip.

"I'll miss him," Frank said. "One of my best customers."

Fenimore's next stop was the Pancoasts' carriage house; a roomy place, large enough to store a sailboat as well as Tom's car. A police officer, who looked no more than sixteen, presided over the site from a beach chair. They recruited them young in Seacrest. Fenimore showed him a slip signed by the Chief of Police.

The car, a neat Porsche, had been gone over with a fine-tooth comb. No evidence of any clutter or debris on the floor, in the side pockets, or even in the glove compartment. In fact, it looked as if it had never left the showroom. "Was the car like this *before* you searched it?"

The boy nodded. "Clean as a whistle. The only things in the glove compartment were the registration, the insurance, and the instruction manual."

Ruefully, Fenimore thought of his own beat-up Chevy and the junk collected in it. Tom must have been one of those car fanatics who had a heart attack over every scratch and stain. Fenimore was about to leave when he noticed a sticker on the back window. The sleek red and black logo of an exclusive squash club. Maybe one of Tom's squash partners could shed more light on Tom. One of the cardinal rules of homicide detection: get to know the victim.

· · ·

The squash court was noisy with resounding thwacks as two relatively young men engaged in a match. Fenimore waited patiently. He had had a hard time getting admitted to the club. Nonmembers in a small town were not looked upon with favor. Not until he placed a call to the Pancoast household and attained Judith's seal of approval had he been allowed entry to the holy sanctuary.

Fenimore had acquired the names of the two men—Josh and Henry—from the club manager. They were both occasional squash opponents of Tom's, the manager assured him. Finally finished, the two men sauntered off the court, wiping their dripping faces with snowy towels provided by the club.

"Pardon me, but—" Fenimore explained his mission.

The two men were suitably shocked at the news of Tom's fate. It is especially hard on young men to hear about the death of a contemporary.

"When did it happen?" asked Josh.

"This afternoon."

They shook their heads.

"Does his wife know?" Henry asked.

"I believe so."

"The poor kids," Josh murmured.

"Did he seem depressed lately?"

They looked at each other.

"No way," Henry said.

"Did he have any enemies?"

"Not *off* the court," Josh said slyly.

Fenimore had a hard time believing that anyone would commit murder over a squash score. "Do you know if he had any major problems? With money, for instance? Or in his marriage?"

At the word "marriage" the two men exchanged a quick look.

"I hear his wife was into psychics and things like that," Fenimore pursued.

"It's a hobby of hers," Henry offered.

"How about his boozing? Did his wife object to that?"

"Not enough to murder him if that's what you're getting at," Josh said.

"He may have overdone the drink, but he wasn't a mean drunk," Henry added.

"In fact, it usually made him the opposite," put in Josh. "Friendlier".

"Can you think of anyone who might have had a grudge against him?"

They shook their heads quickly and in unison.

"He wasn't that kind of guy," Henry said.

Josh nodded in agreement.

Fenimore thanked the two squash players and let them escape to their showers.

Fenimore had saved Mildred for last. He hated to interrogate someone so recently bereaved. But when murder was suspected such niceties could not be indulged. And as every detective knows, the murder victim's mate is always the number one suspect. He had called ahead to warn Mildred of his visit. As he approached the sprawling ranch house he had mixed emotions. A tricycle sat in the driveway and a pair of Roller-blades lay near the front door.

It was Susanne Pancoast who answered his ring. Her face was pale and strained.

"I'm sorry to intrude—"

"That's all right. The police just left. Mildred's expecting you." She led him into a kind of sitting room or den. Mildred Pancoast was hunched over a card table. Some cards were spread out before her. When she looked up, Fenimore was confronted with a face ravaged by weeping.

"I'm terribly sorry to disturb you, Mrs. Pancoast. But we're anxious to get to the bottom of this."

She gestured to a chair, low-slung, made of canvas and iron. When he slid into it, Fenimore found himself almost horizontal to the floor. Not the best position for conducting an interview. Awkwardly, he climbed out and moved to a more standard seat.

"You're that doctor-detective, aren't you?"

He nodded.

"He didn't do it," she said.

"I beg your pardon?"

"Tom wouldn't kill himself."

"What makes you so sure?"

"He wasn't depressed. He never talked about suicide. He didn't leave a note. Besides, he's a . . ." she swallowed, took a deep breath, and went on, "he *was* . . . a Leo. And Leos aren't suicidal."

"I see." Fenimore made a mental note to review the personality traits of the astronomical signs. He was a Pices, himself, and had never liked being born under the sign of a fish. He would have preferred Taurus—or Scorpio, whose traits seemed

much more like his own. "Did your husband have any enemies?" he asked.

"Not that I know of."

"Money problems?"

"Who doesn't?"

"I thought all the Pancoasts were . . . er . . . rather well off."

"There's never enough, you know."

Fenimore didn't know. He had never wanted more. He had
plenty to meet his needs, which, by most doctor's standards,
were small.

"Did you ever hear any of the Pancoasts express a need for
more money?"

"You're not going to get me to point the finger," Mildred
said quickly. "But I've heard all of them say, more than once,
they could use more."

"I see."

"You probably don't see. You don't have kids, do you?"

He shook his head.

"They're what eat it up. The schools, the camps, their teeth,
their lessons—music, tennis, riding, sailing." She ticked them
off on her fingers. "Then there's saving for their colleges. It's
endless."

A child came to the door, sucking her thumb. It was hard
to imagine such a small creature being such a huge burden. Her
face also bore signs of weeping. "Come here, hon." Mildred
beckoned to her. The little girl ran to her mother and buried
her head in her lap.

"Molly!" Susanne appeared in the doorway.

"It's all right, Sue," Mildred said.

But Susanne led Molly away.

It was time to leave, Fenimore decided. He rose and thanked the young widow.

As he headed for the front door, he paused, realizing he had forgotten to ask the key question—what was she doing at the time of the murder? He turned. Susanne was right behind him. "Where was Mildred at the time of Tom's death?" he asked her.

She frowned. "At school. Picking up her children."

"And you?"

"Me?" She was startled.

He nodded.

"The same place. We both have children at the school."

"And your husband?"

"Adam? At school of course. A different school. The Academy. He teaches there."

"Do you have a copy of his course schedule?"

"Not with me," she said shortly.

"Of course not. Could you send me one?"

"I suppose, but—"

"Thank you." Fenimore left hastily. There were times when his hobby left a bad taste in his mouth.

Back in the car, Fenimore pondered what he had learned:

1. Tom had a drinking problem.
2. He was not suicidal.
3. He probably had no serious enemies.

4. He was living beyond his means.

5. All the Pancoasts were living beyond their means.

With the possible exception of the aunts. Although, even they invested heavily in dollhouse furnishings, which could be astronomically expensive. *What was he thinking?* What had the aunts to gain from killing Tom? They were the ones who held the purse strings! His thoughts were getting fuzzy. He switched his attention to alibis. At the time of Pamela's death, all the Pancoasts were gathered in one place, but at the time of Tom's death, they were scattered. Quickly, he drew up a list of their whereabouts:

ALIBIS FOR SUSPECTS IN THE DEATH
OF TOM PANCOAST

Suspect	Alibi	Loophole
Emily	Napping	Could slip down to carriage house at any time
Judith	Shopping	Could sneak back to C. H. at any time
Mildred	Picking up kids at school	It doesn't take an hour to pick up kids. Had thirty minutes to go to C. H.
Susanne	Picking up kids at school	Same as above

SUSPECT	ALIBI	LOOPHOLE
Adam	At Academy	Could have slipped out and gone to C. H. Academy only 3 miles from Seacrest
Edgar	At work on site a few miles from Seacrest	Could have slipped back to C. H. during lunch hour
Marie	Sculpting in studio at Pancoast house	Could have slipped down to C. H. while Emily was napping and Judith was shopping
Carrie	At school, having study hour	Could have slipped out and gone to C. H.
Frank	Bartending	Could have gone to C. H. on his break

12/5 Mildred Pancoast's Diary:

Dear Diary,

*Today we buried Tom. I am a widow and my poor children are fatherless. They say it was suicide. But I don't believe it. He didn't leave a note. And I'm sure he wasn't that unhappy. We still had good times. And there were the children. I blame it on those dolls. Somebody was out to get Tom. And I think it was somebody in the family. They worked their voodoo on him—through his doll. I'm so glad I didn't let the aunts make one of me. At least I'm safe. My children won't be orphans. I wish they'd get rid of all those damned dolls. Drown them, burn them, bury them. Something! I remember that story by Agatha Christie—*And Then There Were None. *Those ten little Indian dolls on the dining room table. Whenever one broke, someone died. I always wondered why someone didn't hide them or smash them, destroy them somehow. They might have prevented all those murders. If we get rid of the dolls, maybe we can prevent more deaths. First Pamela. Now Tom. Who's next?*

CHAPTER 12

The day of the yard sale dawned brisk and bright. It was really a sidewalk sale because Philadelphia town houses are rarely blessed with front yards. Fenimore was in the midst of a lovely dream—walking hand in hand with Jennifer along a beach searching for seashells—when the harsh buzz of the doorbell jarred him awake.

"You're an early bird." Fenimore squinted at Horatio on his front stoop, a dark figure against the bright sunshine.

"Big day, man." He pushed past the pajama-clad doctor and headed for the cellar.

Wearily, Fenimore made his way upstairs to dress for this event that he had been dreading. He had tried to postpone it, advising them that it was the wrong time of year. But Mrs. Doyle had overridden him. "It's just the right time of year," she insisted. "In December, people are always looking for something to put in a stocking or to give to that odd person." Fenimore disliked the term "odd person." Was she implying that only *odd* people would want his things?

He had been ordered to dress appropriately. Not in his accustomed navy suit, white shirt, regimental-striped tie, and black oxfords. He rummaged through his closet, looking for the pair of old trousers he kept on hand for household emergencies, such as tightening a washer, tacking down a linoleum square, or replacing a smoke alarm battery—the full extent of his home maintenance skills.

"Meowrr." His cat Sal had followed him into the closet and Fenimore had inadvertently closed the door on her. He hastily opened the door. The cat rushed out and disappeared under the bed. The first mishap in a day filled with mishaps, he predicted morosely. Sometime later, he reappeared downstairs clad in his old pants, a T-shirt that had been a nice shade of forest green before an overdose of bleach had rendered it a sickly gray, and his "kamikaze" sneakers. (Jennifer had christened them that, because, "Only someone bent on suicide would wear such dreadful things," she said.)

Horatio was attempting to wiggle a battered bureau through the front door.

"Hey," Fenimore stopped him. "Are we sure we want to get rid of that?" Except for a few scratches and a missing drawer it seemed in perfect condition.

"We're sure." Mrs. Doyle came up behind him.

"When did you get here?" Fenimore felt ambushed, surrounded on all sides by the enemy. Even Sal had taken up a post on the stairs, blocking retreat in that direction.

"I've been here since seven—making these." His nurse held out a handful of red stickers, each neatly decorated with a black price mark.

"How did you know what to charge?" Fenimore was mystified.

"Horse sense," she snorted, going to Horatio's aid. Together they shoved the bureau through the doorway and carried it out to the sidewalk.

When Fenimore caught sight of his sidewalk, he was aghast. There was barely room for the skinniest pedestrian to slip between the accumulation of furniture, kitchenware, books, clothing, and knickknacks. Anxiously, he went out to examine his lost wares.

"Don't go takin' anything in again," Horatio warned dangerously.

Plunging his hands conscientiously in his pockets, Fenimore surveyed the motley collection—the doorstop in the shape of an owl, the *Life* magazine displaying Elizabeth Taylor as a teenage bride, the pewter soap dish with the hinged top. He was reaching for the soap dish when Mrs. Doyle slapped a red sticker on it—75¢, it read.

"Seventy-five cents? That belonged to my grandmother!"

"That's all it'll bring," said his nurse, matter-of-factly.

"But the memories . . . ?"

"Of your grandmother washing her hands?"

"Well . . . er . . . yes."

"Oh, very well," she relented, peeling off the sticker. "Now mind, you put that on your bathroom sink and use it every day. If I find it back in the cellar, out it goes."

"Yes, ma'am," he said meekly, snatching up the soap dish and stuffing it into his pocket.

While he perused the rest of the cluttered sidewalk, a woman passerby joined him. They browsed in tandem. "Did you ever see such a collection of junk?" she said, irritably. "People have some nerve trying to palm off stuff that belongs in one place, and one place only—"

Fenimore looked at her.

"The city dump!" she said, and hurried down the street.

Turning toward the house, he caught sight of Mrs. Doyle and Horatio conferring on the front steps. He had never seen such camaraderie between his two employees. Usually at odds, today they seemed in perfect accord. For some reason this unnerved him. After casting a surreptitious glance his way, Mrs. Doyle disappeared inside. Horatio, whistling a tuneless air, rearranged some broken-down chairs that didn't require rearranging. A few minutes later Mrs. Doyle reemerged with a telephone message for Fenimore. Rafferty, his policeman friend, wanted a call. Happy to leave the litter of his past behind, Fenimore went to the phone.

"I've got two tickets to the Eagles game this afternoon. How 'bout it?"

What luck. He could escape this whole depressing business. "Great!"

"See you at Gate D, at one o'clock."

It wasn't until the second half that it occurred to Fenimore to ask Rafferty, "Where did you get these tickets?"

"Your nurse called. Told me to pick them up at the box office. Damned nice of her to include me."

Fenimore fidgeted and squirmed through the rest of the game.

When he turned into Spruce Street, he began to trot. When he saw the empty sidewalk in front of his house, his panic grew. The interior of the house was ominously silent. Even Sal wasn't there to greet him. With foreboding, he glanced in the waiting room. All the furniture seemed to be intact. After a quick survey of the inner office, he sighed with relief. Nothing missing there. His heart palpitated as he opened the cellar door and flicked on the light. Seven hundred square feet of immaculate concrete stretched before him. He could walk from one end of the cellar to the other unimpeded. But it wasn't until he ran his hand over the top of the hot water heater that he was really impressed. No dust.

As he made his way up the cellar stairs, Sal was waiting for him at the top. At least they hadn't sold her! He scooped her up and carried her over to his favorite armchair. Taped to its leather back was an envelope with his name on it. Letting Sal slide to the cushioned seat, he tore open the envelope. Two crisp, new, twenty-dollar bills fell into his hand, followed by a quarter, a nickel, and two pennies. Tucked inside was a note in Mrs. Doyle's precise penmanship: "Your cut (minus the cost of two Eagles tickets.)"

CHAPTER 13

Since the loss of two children, in less than a month, Marie Pancoast's personality had undergone a dramatic change. Once cheerful and outgoing, she was now quick-tempered and withdrawn. Before, her family had been the focus of her universe, and sculpting a mere hobby or pastime. Now, she was hardly aware of her family (what remained of it) and sculpting occupied all her waking hours. She spent more and more time in her studio. The only way she could cope with her loss was to immerse herself in her work. When she was shaping a block of wood or stone into some intelligible form, she could bury her pain. But as soon as she stopped, it rushed back all the stronger for having been forgotten for a time.

As a result, she worked until she was exhausted, sometimes forgetting to eat or sleep. Often she slept on a cot that she kept in the studio for that purpose. Edgar was also distraught: torn between grieving over the loss of his children and watching the transformation of his wife. He neglected his work and began to lose clients. Other architectural firms outbid him and succeeded in meeting the deadlines that he no longer cared about. He spent his days in the aunts' parlor staring at the newspaper, rarely turning a page. Every now and then, he would go up to the studio and beg his wife to come down and eat something or come home with him and sleep.

The aunts clucked over their brother continually, bringing him tea and coffee and treats to tempt him back into life. Susanne, the only remaining child, dropped by every day to see her parents and try to comfort them. Sometimes she brought the children, hoping to distract them. But they barely acknowledged Amanda and Tad, and it was usually left to the aunts to entertain them.

One day, a particularly pathetic ceremony took place in the garden. Mildred Pancoast had convinced the aunts that the dolls were in some way responsible for the tragedies. She insisted—in quite a hysterical scene—that they destroy them.

"If only you'd get rid of those damned dolls, there wouldn't be any more deaths," she screamed at the shaken aunts. (No one in the family could bring themselves to refer to the deaths as "murders" yet.)

Although failing to see the logic of her request, out of deference to the poor widow's wishes, the aunts agreed to dispose of the dolls—and their clothes. Each doll had an intricately made wardrobe for every season of the year. It was especially painful to Emily to part with her doll's tiny fringed shawl, which bore a delicate butterfly embroidered on the back. And it nearly broke Judith's heart to give up her doll's miniature pair of black patent leather boots.

They chose a particularly blustery December day for this doleful task. Both wore overcoats. Judith wore a felt hat pulled down over her fuzzy curls and Emily tied a wool scarf under her chin. Judith carried the spade. Emily carried two shoe boxes—one filled with the dolls, the other with their clothes.

Judith tried to press the spade into the ground, but the earth was like stone. She could hardly make a dent in it. Emily offered to try, but Judith forbade it, remembering her sister's heart. Judith prowled around the garden, searching for a hole or crevice among the bare hydrangea bushes or in the dried-up vegetable patch. She paused at the bottom of the garden and beckoned to Emily. She had found a cavity—a sort of depression in the earth—possibly made by some animal. Judith directed Emily to lay the shoe boxes in it. Emily obeyed. Judith prowled the garden again until she found some loose soil and small stones she could pick up easily with her shovel. She had to make several trips back and forth, dropping the material on the shoe boxes, to cover them completely. When they were no longer visible, Emily pulled some weeds and dead grass over them for good measure. They lingered before starting back to the house, both feeling that something was missing. But what? A prayer? That hardly seemed suitable. Slowly, their heads bent against the wind, they made their way back to the house.

As they approached the back steps, Emily was in the lead. There was a hole in the bottom step where the wood had rotted away. Under normal circumstances, Edgar would have repaired it by now. But he had repaired nothing recently. And they had forgotten to tell Adam about it. Suddenly Emily's leg gave way under her and she let out a sharp cry. She had caught her foot in the hole and fallen. Judith dropped the spade and ran for help.

By teatime Emily was in the Emergency Room of the Seacrest Hospital awaiting surgery. X rays had revealed a broken hip. Most of the Pancoast family was gathered in the lobby, their heavier sorrows overshadowed for the moment by this new emergency. Judith was allowed to stay with Emily until she was taken to the operating room, but she stepped into the lobby briefly to telephone Fenimore about the accident.

When the phone rang, Mrs. Doyle answered it. When she told Fenimore it was Judith Pancoast, his stomach contracted. Upon learning the reason for her call, he was almost relieved that it was nothing worse.

"Who is the cardiologist in charge?" he asked sharply.

"Dr. Lukens."

"Ask him to call me right away. I want to fill him in on Emily's cardiologic history."

"Yes, Doctor."

Later, when Emily was safely in the recovery room, Judith called the doctor again to tell him the operation was a success.

"Well, that *is* good news!" He nodded vigorously in answer to Mrs. Doyle's gesticulated question. "Tell Emily I'll come down next week to cheer her up."

"Oh, would you, Doctor? We do need cheering up. We just buried the dolls and all their clothes."

"You what?"

"Well, Mildred felt the dolls were somehow to blame for our recent troubles, so we thought the best thing to do was bury them in the garden. That's how Emily had her accident."

"My word." Fenimore paused, overcome by the enormity of his friends' sacrifice. "Well, leave it to me. I'll think of something. Have there been any other odd occurrences—connected with the dollhouse, I mean?"

"No, nothing like that."

"Have the police been bothering you?"

"Not recently. But I suppose they'll be back." Judith sighed.

"You can count on it. Well, give my best to Emily when she wakes up."

Fenimore replaced the receiver and glanced over at Mrs. Doyle. Once she had heard the good news about Emily, she had gone back to work feverishly at her desk. Tonight was the third meeting of RUB—the karate class she had been conducting in his cellar. She was outlining the lesson for that night. When he asked Mrs. Doyle how her students were progressing, she had laughed menacingly. "I pity the first mugger who tackles one of my graduates," she said grimly. "He'll rue the day!"

"And who is your best pupil?" asked Fenimore curiously.

"Oh, Amelia Dunwoody, without a doubt. She nearly knocked Mabel Parsons out with her karate chop."

Fenimore shook his head. He felt almost sorry for those poor unsuspecting muggers lying innocently in wait for this band of little old ladies. Obviously, they would be no match for a member of the Red Umbrella Brigade.

The doctor went back to pondering how he might cheer up the Pancoast sisters.

In a flash, it came to him.

CHAPTER 14

Mrs. Doyle shepherded her band of students into the rented van and they all settled back to enjoy the scenery. It was the second Saturday in December and by some miracle all the members of the karate class had been able to adjust their Christmas shopping schedules to make the trip to Seacrest. Horatio's help had also been enlisted. He had rolled up the mats and tied them to the luggage rack on top of the van. As a reward, he had been invited to see the performance. As he sat huddled in the backseat, as far away from the cackling women as possible, he had mixed feelings about the invitation. Dr. Fenimore was at the wheel.

"Now, Amelia . . ." Mrs. Doyle had arranged to sit next to her prize pupil in order to give her some final instructions. "Be careful with your karate chop, we don't want to hospitalize any of the ladies right before Christmas."

"I've never been to the Shore in December," said Mabel Parsons.

"You won't catch her taking a swim, I'll bet," said another octogenarian.

"Why not?" retorted Amelia. "When my husband and I were younger we belonged to the Polar Bear Club and went in the surf every January."

"Brrrr," said Mrs. Doyle. "Better you than me."

Fenimore found driving an unfamiliar vehicle arduous, especially to the background noise of the ladies' endless chatter. Reminding himself that it was for a good cause, he gritted his teeth and concentrated on the road ahead. Fortunately, in December, the road to the Shore had very little traffic.

"Oh, look, Kathleen! There's a scarecrow."

Mrs. Doyle looked out her window. Sure enough, a jaunty scarecrow stood guard over a desolate field of withered corn stalks.

"He looks just like Horatio!" someone cried.

Shrieks of laughter greeted this pronouncement.

If the van window had not been sealed shut, Horatio would have jumped out then and there.

Fenimore sincerely hoped that the Pancoast sisters appreciated the sacrifice he was making on their behalf.

As they pulled up to the Victorian mansion, it began to rain. This was a cause of consternation to the party. Mrs. Doyle had planned to present her performance outside on the front lawn.

"What on earth shall we do?" she whispered over Fenimore's shoulder.

"Don't panic. The Pancoasts' dining room is big enough to accomodate a Flyers game. With a little shuffling of furniture, we'll manage."

"Here they come, Emily!" Judith called her sister to the front window. Emily, ensconced in a wheelchair, rolled forward. Fenimore had called the night before to alert them to the impending invasion.

"What pretty sweat suits," Judith observed as the ladies descended from the van in varying shades of pastel pink, blue, yellow, and green. "They look like a bunch of Easter eggs."

"That would make Dr. Fenimore the Easter Bunny," commented Emily dryly.

With Horatio's help, moving the dining room furniture against the wall was easy. The only problem was the china closet. Mrs. Doyle was afraid one of the performers might strike the glass and shatter its priceless contents. Horatio finally solved this problem by tying two wrestling mats over the front of the closet.

At last they were ready to begin. Folding chairs had been erected around the periphery of the room for the audience, which consisted of Judith, Emily , Edgar, Marie, Susanne, and Mildred. Adam and the children were expected to join them later, in time for the finale. Carrie and her little charges had also been invited. Mrs. Doyle had even provided a small tape recorder to play music during the program. It alternated between brisk Sousa marches and soothing Strauss waltzes.

As the music started up, the ladies were all crowded into the kitchen giggling in anticipation of their first performance. They had shed their pastel-colored sweat suits to reveal bright red body suits and leotards, cinched at the waist with their idea of the prestigious "black belt." As the first group of five ladies paraded into the dining room to the beat of "The Washington Post March," Dr. Fenimore knew he had come up with the right tonic for his depressed friends. He glanced over at Horatio. The boy's dark face had deepened a few shades and he was viciously biting his lip. Fenimore prayed this self-inflicted pain would prevent him from erupting into an embarrassing guffaw.

The karate experts lined up in five rows of five each and began their maneuvers. Shaking their fists first to the right, then to the left, they punctuated each move with staccato shouts. The kicks were next, aimed at the audience and accompanied by more shouts. Originally, Fenimore had thought of these women as sort of senior Rockettes. But that image quickly faded. There was nothing merry and bright about these performers. They were in deadly earnest. Their enemies had better watch out.

Refreshments were served after the performance. The ladies had all showered and changed back into their colorful pant suits. Seated in the parlor, balancing their teacups and taking dainty bites of pastries, no one would have suspected them of being able to fend off the fiercest attackers on a dark street corner.

Fenimore set about the other task for which he had come to Seacrest—testing Emily's pacemaker. He had brought the programmer. He unzipped the plastic case and took it out, along with the instruction manual (in case he forgot how it worked). The programmer resembled a laptop computer, but a little larger. Several people gathered around to look—Adam, Susanne, Carrie, Horatio, and a few of the younger children.

"How does it work?" asked Carrie.

Fenimore explained that he programmed the pacemaker to take over Emily's heartbeat if her natural pacemaker failed. To prevent her from becoming dizzy her heart must beat at a rate above fifty-five beats per minute. If it dropped below that, not enough blood would get to her head or other parts of her body, and she would become dizzy or faint.

Mildred wandered over holding the cell phone she seemed never to be without.

"Hey, keep that phone away from here," Fenimore warned. "They've been known to interfere with pacemakers," he said sternly.

Mildred moved away, looking hurt.

As Fenimore beckoned to Emily, he noticed Carrie and Horatio hovering awkwardly in the background. Why not invite them to watch?

"Would you mind if Carrie and Horatio look on?" he asked Emily.

"Heavens no."

"You two wait here until I call you," he said, and pushed Emily in her wheelchair to the privacy of the library.

Fenimore quickly attached three electrodes to Emily's chest and waited while she rebuttoned her blouse. "Come in you two scientists," he called. He lifted the lid of the programmer and the screen glowed amber.

As he adjusted the settings, Emily asked the teenagers, "How would you like to have your life depend on a metal gizmo no bigger than a half dollar?"

"Not much," Horatio said honestly.

Carrie nodded in agreement.

The three watched the screen intently.

"Is everything in order, Doctor?" asked Emily.

Fenimore nodded. "Everything's perfect," he said. "You'll probably be around for another hundred years."

"I hope not." Emily laughed.

As they were leaving the room, Horatio hung back. "What's that?" He pointed to a small box next to Emily's telephone. Carrie lingered too.

"That's a telephone transmitter. Emily wets the index finger of each hand—"

"Sometimes I just stick them in my mouth," Emily said with a twinkle.

"—and inserts each finger into a special ring. Each ring is attached to a lead that, in turn, is plugged into the transmitter. When Emily punches in the pacemaker company's eight-hundred number, her electrocardiogram is sent to them like a fax. The company checks it out every three months to make sure her pacemaker is working."

An hour later the ladies had said their good-byes and were safely packed in the van. Fenimore was about to get in when he remembered Horatio. The last time he had seen him, the boy was tying the mats to the luggage rack. Now there was no sign of him. Fenimore asked everyone, and finally Amelia Dunwoody said she thought she had seen him heading toward the beach.

Fenimore hurried that way. The beach was about a hundred

yards below the back of the Pancoast house and he had to climb through prickly underbrush and over heavy sand dunes to reach it. His oxfords were not made for that kind of excursion. He slipped and slid and the sand poured into his shoes. "Darn that kid," he muttered as he came out onto the beach. It was deserted except for a small figure standing by the water's edge.

Fenimore began hallooing and waving his arms.

Horatio looked up. Slowly he started toward him.

"We're leaving. I couldn't find you," Fenimore complained as the boy drew near.

"I never saw it before," Horatio said.

"What?"

"The ocean."

"Oh." Fenimore was thoughtful as he followed the boy back to the van.

It wasn't until Fenimore was turning into Spruce Street that he remembered the programmer. In all the excitement he had left it behind.

CHAPTER 15

Fenimore had been asleep no more than an hour when he was awakened by the doorbell. He entered the vestibule cautiously and peered through the frosted glass of the front door. (One night he had opened the door too quickly and been attacked by two thugs.) Horatio peered back. Hadn't he just said good night to that kid?

"It's my mom. She's sick."

He let him in. "I'll get my instruments."

"No briefcase."

Fenimore went to the kitchen and reached behind the refrigerator, where he kept a supply of grocery sacks. While transferring his things from his briefcase to the sack he questioned Horatio.

"What's wrong with her?"

"This morning she just had a bad cold. But tonight, when I got home, she could hardly breathe."

"Why didn't you call nine-one-one?" He was alarmed.

"No way. They won't come to our neighborhood." Horatio danced from one foot to the other. "I shouldn't of left her for so long."

With a twinge, Fenimore realized he was to blame. If he hadn't dragged Horatio to Seacrest, the boy would have been home much earlier. Into the paper bag, Fenimore dumped stethoscope, blood pressure cuff, sterile cotton balls, syringes, a vial of penicillin, tongue blades, a bottle of alcohol, a thermometer, and a collection of samples of pills. "Let's go."

Horatio glanced at Fenimore's bare feet.

"Wait a minute." The doctor pattered up the stairs and returned in a few minutes, fully dressed.

Horatio ran out ahead of him. As he locked the front door, Fenimore said, "My car's over there."

"No car," Horatio said. "You want it stripped?"

"But we're in a hurry. . . ."

"Follow me." Swiftly Horatio led the way through the dark streets. Philadelphia streets form a grid pattern. They are perfectly straight and intersect at ninety-degree angles. William Penn laid them out that way in 1682, and nobody had seen fit to change them. It was a boring plan, but easy to follow. The blocks were long, and after midnight, during the week, except for an occasional siren, they were country quiet. But not country safe. Street lamps sprayed light on every corner, turning the spaces in between a deeper dark. Horatio stayed close to the curb, away from alleys and cul-de-sacs. Sometimes he even walked in the middle of the street. Fenimore followed.

Gradually the trees and row houses petered out and were replaced by vacant lots. Fenimore wondered why Horatio hadn't buried his cat somewhere here. (That was how he had first met the boy, when he was trying, unsuccessfully, to bury his cat.) Fenimore asked him.

"And let the hoods dig him up and play catch with him?"

They were now passing vacant lots, and more sky was visible. Not a friendly, star-winking sky. A leaden, smog-heavy sky that weighed on them like a lid. The disappearance of the trees and houses made Fenimore feel vulnerable. He half expected a crop duster to show up and start swooping down at them, like in *North by Northwest*. But Horatio danced on. Fenimore had to push to keep up with him.

They were heading toward a complex of high-rises; three concrete towers loomed dark against the lighter sky. Public housing projects—the government's inspired solution for sheltering the poor.

When they were half a block from the towers, Horatio stopped and turned. "Keep low and close to me. We're going in the back."

Fenimore could make out a group of kids in front, sitting on the ground, leaning against the wall, resting against their bikes. A silvery haze hovered above their heads and the sweetish scent of marijuana reached them. They looked harmless enough, but Horatio knew better. He led Fenimore around the side of the building, careful not to attract their attention.

"Do they ever come after you?" Fenimore resisted a strong urge to glance over his shoulder.

The boy shrugged. "I'm learnin' a few karate moves. Come on," he ordered.

When Horatio leaned on the heavy fire door there was the

sound of scuffling on the other side. "Fuck off!" a voice barked. Horatio ducked around the corner, sped along a cinder-block wall, and stopped before another graffiti-covered door. Fenimore caught up with him as he pushed it—more cautiously this time. No sound. Like a well-trained bloodhound, the boy sniffed before bounding up the concrete fire stairs. The litter on the stairs was ankle-deep. They waded through it. The smell of urine was overwhelming. After four flights of steps, Fenimore was ready to die. He lagged a full flight behind Horatio. His chest burning, he leaned against the wall.

"Come on!"

The boy's harsh whisper urged him upward. At the top of the fifth flight, he could see the boy's silhouette holding the fire door for him.

"This is it." Horatio walked a few feet down the dim corridor and stopped at the first door on the right. His key rasped in the lock.

When Fenimore stepped into the room he stopped short. Confronting him on the opposite wall was his own poster. The stirring scene entitled "The Doctor."

"Mom, I'm back. I brought the doctor." Horatio went over to the open sofa bed which filled most of the room. "Mom!" he shook her.

Fenimore nudged him aside and bent to look. The woman lay buried under a mound of ragged blankets, quilts, over-coats—all scrupulously clean, smelling faintly of camphor. Her face, the only visible part of her, was flushed and moist with perspiration. Her mass of dark hair—the one feature she shared with her son—spread across the pillow. In every other respect, she was the image of a colleen from County Cork. Horatio, on the other hand, resembled a young matador from Madrid. Her name, Horatio had told him, was Bridget. Bridget Lopez.

"Mrs. Lopez?"

She muttered something unintelligible, her eyes closed. Reaching under the covers, Fenimore searched for her hand. He located it by its heat. When he took her pulse, her skin burned under his fingers. She began to cough. The covers shook with each spasm. While waiting for it to subside, Fenimore opened the paper bag and took out a vial of penicillin. "Get me a glass of water and a bowl of ice," he ordered. "And chop the ice."

"What do I chop it with?"

"A hammer, your shoe, anything. Wrap the cubes in a dish towel first."

As soon as Horatio was gone, Fenimore began peeling back the bedclothes. When he reached the woman, he found she was fully dressed in slacks and several layers of sweaters. A vain attempt to ward off chills. Gently, but firmly, he forced a tongue depressor between her teeth and pried her mouth open. With a small flashlight he checked her throat and tonsils. They were badly infected. He undid the sweaters and pressed the stethoscope against her bare chest. As he thought, she had pneumonia.

"Thunk, thunk." Horatio was making progress with the ice.

Fenimore turned the woman, pulled down her slacks, and inserted the needle of the syringe into her buttock. When the boy came back with the water and the ice, his mother was tucked neatly under the covers again.

"Thanks. Put them down and give me a hand. I want to raise your mother a little." Together they managed to raise her to a semi-sitting position. Fenimore took the glass and pressed it to her lips. They were dry and peeling, as if badly sunburned. She opened her eyes and tried to drink. The effort was too much and the water ran down her chin. She brushed it away with her hand and sank back, eyes closed. In a minute they would have to try again.

Fenimore glanced around the room. Except for the open bed, it was neat and tidy: an oasis in the midst of chaos. White curtains hung at the single window. A table was covered with a blue-and-white-checked cloth—a bowl of fruit resting on it. Suddenly Fenimore asked, "Where is everybody?"

"Huh?" Horatio's eyes were fixed on his mother's face.

"Your brothers and sisters? Where are they? Why aren't they here looking after her?" Horatio had told Fenimore he was one of six.

"Oh," he shrugged, "they're probably at my aunt's."

"Where is that?"

"South Thirteenth. She has a garden apartment." He rolled his eyes. "It's just another project, but she has a window box and a flower bed. She can't plant anything in them, 'cause the hoods'll pull 'em up, but she thinks she's better off. She wants us to move over there. She's praying somebody'll get shot or OD and there'll be a vacancy."

"Couldn't one of them have stayed with your mother?"

"She probably shooed them out. She wouldn't want them to catch it. 'They might miss some school.' She's big on school."

This whispered conversation had been carried on over Mrs.

Lopez's prostrate form. Suddenly she opened her eyes. They were the color of the sea under a cloudless sky. Her son's deep brown eyes must have been a gift from his father. Mr. Lopez had been shot by a random bullet while he was sitting on his front porch. "Killed for the sin of wanting a breath of fresh air," his wife said. That's why they'd moved to the project. Mrs. Lopez thought it would be safer.

"That you, Ray?"

He moved closer. "Yeah. I brought the doctor. You know, the one I work for."

Curiosity gave her strength. She turned her head to look at Fenimore.

"Hello, ma'am. You're going to be okay. I gave you a shot of penicillin and I think it's beginning to work." (It couldn't possibly begin to work for another twelve hours, but it would help her to think it would.) "Come on, Rat. Let's try that water again."

Horatio raised his mother's head and Fenimore put the glass to her lips. This time she took some and swallowed it. When she had drunk half the contents, she pushed it away and glared at her son. "What're you doing here? Wanna catch something?"

Horatio sent Fenimore a what-did-I-tell-you look.

"Your son did the right thing, ma'am. You're very sick. Someone has to look after you." As he spoke, she suddenly began to cough—each heave wracking her whole body. When it stopped, she fell back and didn't try to talk again.

Fenimore poured some penicillin tablets into a plastic bottle and instructed Horatio on the dosage. He also gave him a bottle of cough medicine. "This has codeine in it. Give her one teaspoon now, and another if she starts to cough again. Try to get her to drink, but if she won't, get her to suck ice. You better put that ice back in the freezer now." He began to pack up his instruments. "If she isn't better by noon tomorrow, call me and we'll get her to the hospital." He looked around for the phone.

"We don't have one," Horatio said.

"Is there a pay phone in the building?"

He snorted. "They rip 'em out as soon as they put 'em in. But there's one at the deli a few blocks away. The dealers use it."

"Okay. And no school tomorrow. If they want a note, refer them to me." He spoke to the woman. "Mrs. Lopez, I've asked your son to stay home tomorrow and look after you. Those are doctor's orders."

She didn't open her eyes or make any further protest.

"Man, she *is* sick." Horatio looked alarmed.

"She'll be okay," Fenimore reassured him, "but you have to stay with her."

"But I hafta walk you home."

"No way," he adopted the boy's expression. "I'll be fine."

"You'll never make it." He looked him over. "You never would've made it here without me. At least you're not wearing a fuckin' tie." He unbuttoned the two top buttons of Fenimore's shirt, revealing a white undershirt, and pulled the collar of his jacket up. Still dissatisfied, he grabbed a cap off a hook on the wall—a kind of Andy Capp affair. "Put it on."

Fenimore obeyed.

"That's better. I'll see you outta here." His expression was mulish and Fenimore decided not to protest. Before he opened the door, Horatio glanced back at his mother. She seemed to be resting comfortably. As he stepped out, he darted a look up and down the corridor. "Come on." But he carefully locked the door behind them.

They took the corridor in short bursts, stopping every few yards to listen. The concrete walls echoed with a fight, a staccato exchange of obscenities. They passed two kids helping each other with their heroin shots; bumped into a couple in a deep embrace plastered against the wall; and tripped over a drunk sprawled on the third-floor landing. None of these occupants noticed them. When they reached the ground floor, Horatio shoved the door open. Again he sniffed like a bloodhound seeking the trail. Fenimore sniffed for another reason—to replace the noxious odors of the fire stairs with some relatively fresh air.

"Looks okay"—he turned to Fenimore—"but I don't like it. Remember, keep low." He gave him a gentle shove.

As Fenimore made his way across the vacant lot, "keeping low," he experienced déjà vu. When had he last covered ground in a similar manner? Then he remembered—'69, in Nam.

CHAPTER 16

Every year, on the Saturday before Christmas, it was the custom for the Pancoast sisters to have an open house and display the dollhouse. It was always beautifully decorated, inside and out, just like their real house. It had a wreath on the door, a tree in the parlor with tiny colored lights (that actually blinked), and a stocking for each member of the family hanging from the mantelpiece. Of course, in the dining room, the table was set with a traditional roast of beef and plum pudding (sculpted from polymer and exquisitely painted by Marie).

The inhabitants of Seacrest, adults as well as children, looked forward eagerly to this party every year. Next to Christmas itself, it was the most important event of the season. But this year, for obvious reasons, the aunts were in no mood for a party. They had definitely agreed not to have it.

One afternoon the doorbell rang. It was Carrie. She was just passing by and thought she'd stop in to ask when they expected her to come serve the refreshments at the open house.

Emily and Judith were silent as Carrie looked from one to the other. Finally, Judith said, "Well, dear, we thought we wouldn't have an open house this year."

"Not have it? Oh, Miss Judith, what will I do? The children look forward to it so. It's the only Christmas celebration they have, except for the few little presents I can dig up for them at the thrift shop. And they love the dollhouse. It won't be Christmas if they don't see the dollhouse all lighted up. What on earth will I tell them?"

Emily coughed and shifted in her wheelchair. Judith played with her rings and looked out the window.

"And what about all the others?" Carrie went on. "The whole town comes to your open house. They'll be so disappointed. It will ruin everybody's Christmas." She stopped suddenly, afraid she had gone too far.

Emily looked over at Judith. "I suppose it is selfish to let our unhappiness spoil everyone else's happiness."

Slowly Judith nodded. "It does seem mean to deny them a party—especially the children."

"Oh, Miss Judith! Miss Emily! Thank you! Don't worry about a thing. I'll do everything. Just give me the list. I'll buy the groceries. I'll set the table. I'll even trim the tree, if you'd like. . . ."

The aunts thanked her and told her they'd call her as soon as their plans were firm. As they watched her from the window—she was almost skipping down the path—they agreed they had done the right thing.

When Dr. Fenimore received his annual Christmas greeting card from the Pancoasts, he was surprised to see that it included an invitation to their traditional open house. Last year he had attended with Jennifer and it had been a happy occasion. But this year was quite a different matter. Of course, he would go. It would be a perfect opportunity to observe the Pancoast family members closely. Since Jennifer was still in France, he decided to take Mrs. Doyle.

When they arrived at the Pancoast house, the long driveway was already filled with cars and they had to park in the street. Mrs. Doyle was thrilled by the decorations. In each window burned a single white candle in a nest of holly with white berries. Fixed to the door was an arrangement of pine boughs gathered together with a white satin bow and hung with cones. White had been substituted for the usual red, Fenimore surmised, in deference to the recently departed family members.

The door opened to his touch revealing a long line of people facing toward the foot of the central staircase where the dollhouse stood in all its splendor. The young woman in front of them turned. It was Carrie.

"Oh, hello, Doctor." She smiled. "I'm taking the kids through now because I have to serve the refreshments later."

Her brothers and sisters had all been scrubbed and brushed and dressed in their Sunday best for the occasion. They were also on their best behavior. They stood patiently in line in front of Carrie, their excitement only evident in their faces as they turned occasionally to make sure their sister was still there.

The line progressed slowly. While they waited, Fenimore introduced Carrie to Mrs. Doyle and they chatted. When Carrie found out that Mrs. Doyle was a nurse, her face lit up. "Oh, that's what I wanted to be," she said.

"Why the past tense?" asked Fenimore.

Her smile faded. "Oh well, it's impossible now—since mother's . . . uh . . . illness."

"But there are things you can do at home," Mrs. Doyle said. "Correspondence courses, for instance. That's how I got my start."

Fenimore looked at his nurse. He had not known that.

"My father was a chronic invalid and I was needed at home too. I'll send you some information about those courses."

"Oh, would you, Mrs. Doyle? I'd be so grateful." Then she turned to Fenimore with an anxious expression. "The police have been to see me three times, Doctor. They keep harping on the fact that I was in the kitchen on Thanksgiving. . . ."

"Jackasses!" Fenimore barked so loudly that several people turned to look at him. "Don't worry about it. I'll have a word with them before I go back."

They were approaching the dollhouse at last and Carrie's attention was distracted by her brothers and sisters as they begged her to look at "the tiny tree!" and "the little stockings!" and "the plum pudding!"

The next time they saw Carrie, she was wearing a white frilly apron and offering them an assortment of Christmas cookies on a tray. "Aren't they pretty?" she said.

They each took one and she moved on.

"Nice child," Mrs. Doyle said.

Fenimore told her the nature of Carrie's mother's illness.

The nurse shook her head. "I'll send her that information right away. She can begin to learn the fundamentals at home and get her hands-on experience later. She'd make a fine nurse. I can tell. She has all the right instincts."

"Doctor, may I have a word with you?" It was Adam Turner, the school teacher.

"Certainly. What's up?"

"The police," Adam said. "They've been pestering us day and night. It's interfering with my work. And Susanne's at her wit's end."

"They've even been badgering the children." Susanne joined them and nodded at Amanda and Tad, who were stuffing themselves with petit fours nearby.

At least Carrie wasn't their only suspect. Fenimore was relieved. And secretly, he was pleased the police were doing their job. "I plan to talk to them this afternoon," he said. Which was true, but for other reasons.

"We'd appreciate that," Adam said.

During the course of the party, Fenimore was accosted by each member of the Pancoast family, except Marie, who had declined to come. Edgar, Mildred, Judith, and Emily all complained bitterly about being visited and questioned frequently by the local police, and usually at the most inopportune times— while at dinner, asleep, or in the bath. Mildred was the most indignant. She had been soaking in a bubble bath studying her horoscope, trying to soothe her jagged nerves, when who should ring the bell but some cop and his smart aleck sidekick who took notes on every word she said. She had barely had time to put on a dressing gown before they barged in. And would you believe, they even questioned the children. There ought to be a law.

Exasperated, Fenimore said, "You should be glad they're trying to enforce the law." With a dark look, Mildred stalked off. A very becoming pink shawl lightened her widow's weeds today, Fenimore noticed.

"What was her problem?" asked Mrs. Doyle.

He told her. "Would you mind if I deserted you to pay a call on the Seacrest Police? I want to see how they're getting on. I won't be long."

"Go ahead. I'm enjoying myself."

Mrs. Doyle was an easy mixer. It wasn't long before she had engaged all the Pancoasts in conversation and formed her own opinion of each of them. None of them had impressed her as a murderer. But then, she was the first to acknowledge that the most unlikely people fall into that category. Reserving judgment, she decided it was time for another cup of punch. The punch bowl was located down the hall from the dollhouse. For the second time that day, she regretted its blandness. A splash of vodka or rum would have improved it immensely. (Actually, what she really craved was a cold beer.)

The line to the dollhouse had long since dispersed and some children were examining it. They had been sternly admonished to *look, not touch*. Suddenly one child let out a sharp cry and pointed to the attic. Mrs. Doyle came to see.

The attic was outfitted like a sculptor's studio down to the smallest detail. Under a tiny skylight there were pieces of miniature sculpture in various stages of development—finished, half finished, and just begun. Tiny sculptor's tools—a hammer, chisels, and a blowtorch—were neatly spread out on a wooden bench. On the floor, beside the bench, lay what appeared to be a wooden figure wearing a long white apron—the kind a sculptor might wear to protect her clothes while working. Upon closer examination, Mrs. Doyle saw that the figure had been fashioned from a clothespin. Next to the clothespin lay a plaster cast—the bust of some personage. She couldn't identify it because it was split in half. She turned to the little boy who had cried out. "Did you do that?"

His lower lip trembled. "No. Honest. It was that way when I came." The other children nodded emphatically, assuring her that what he said was true.

"Sorry, dear." Mrs. Doyle remembered the doctor telling her that Marie Pancoast was a sculptor and she now realized that Marie was the only member of the family she had not seen that day. She darted up the stairs. If she met anyone she could always say she was looking for the bathroom. Finding no one on the second floor, she made her way to the third. At the top of the stairs she stopped before a closed door. Hanging from the knob dangled a small sign: DO NOT DISTURB. Not easily intimidated, Mrs. Doyle knocked loudly. No answer. She knocked again and called, "Mrs. Pancoast? Are you all right?"

The door flew open. "Can't you read?" Marie glared.

"Oh, please forgive me. . . ."

"What do you want?"

"I didn't see you downstairs and I just wondered . . ."

"I told the aunts I'd only make a brief appearance. I think it was very thoughtless of them to have the party at all—under the circumstances. Now, if you don't mind, I'll get back to my work." She didn't exactly slam the door, but she closed it very firmly.

Mrs. Doyle retraced her steps, face flaming.

CHAPTER 17

When Mrs. Doyle reached the first floor she went to look for Dr. Fenimore. He hadn't returned from town. Most of the guests had left and it was growing dark. Through the window she glimpsed an orange moon the size of a beach ball rising over the sea. No one else took any notice of it. When you live in such a setting all the time, she supposed, you take the beauty for granted. Judith interrupted her musings to ask if she would like a cup of tea.

"That would be nice."

The two sisters had known Mrs. Doyle for years as a result of their office visits to Dr. Fenimore and they were fond of her. Soon she and Emily and Judith were comfortably settled in a corner of the parlor, chatting. Carrie, finished with her cleaning up, stopped by on her way out to give Mrs. Doyle her address. She begged her not to forget to send the information about the correspondence course.

"What are you going to send her?" Because of her poor hearing, Emily had missed some of the conversation.

Mrs. Doyle told her about Carrie's ambition to become a nurse.

"Well, good luck to her," Emily said. "I wanted to be a doctor, but my father wouldn't hear of it."

"Times are different now, Emily," Judith observed. "Women do what they want." Mrs. Doyle detected a wistful note in her voice.

When her sister left the room to refill the teapot, Emily spoke in a low tone to Mrs. Doyle. "Judith was once engaged to a seaman. Our father forbade her to marry him. It nearly broke her heart."

When Judith reappeared with the pot, Emily said, "Shouldn't we ask Marie to join us?"

"I don't think she wants to be disturbed." Mrs. Doyle was emphatic.

"Oh, of course. I forgot she was working."

"Not all women were stay-at-homes in the old days." Judith returned to their former topic. "We had one ancestor who went to sea with her husband, remember, Emily?"

"Oh yes. Rebecca. She kept a journal. We have it in the attic somewhere. She tells tales of pirates and mutiny. She's the one who brought back the ruby—"

But Judith's tale of the ruby was interrupted by the return of Dr. Fenimore. He apologized for his long absence. As soon as Mrs. Doyle could get his attention, she drew him aside and told him about the scene in the dollhouse.

"Where is Marie now?" He scanned the room.

"In her studio."

He gave her a sharp look.

"No, it's all right. I checked. She's very much alive." Mrs. Doyle reddened at the memory of her reception.

"Nevertheless, I think I'll have a look," Fenimore hurried out.

"Good luck," Mrs. Doyle called after him.

Fenimore paused in the hall to examine the carefully contrived scene in the dollhouse studio. Then he bounded up the stairs, taking them two at a time.

On the third floor, he went through the same routine as Mrs. Doyle had done. But unlike his nurse, his knocks went unanswered. He tried the knob. The door opened. The room was brilliant. Not with electric light, but with moonlight—pouring through the skylight. It turned everything black and white, like an old film.

"Mrs. Pancoast?" His eyes slid nervously around the room. Perhaps she had gone home. He stepped inside and spotted her—spread-eagled beside her workbench. Near her head lay a white bust. The bust was split in half and spattered with a black substance. He fumbled for the light switch. When he found it, the black substance became red.

... and hit it with the tongs and with the shovel—
bang, bang, smash, smash!

—*The Tale of Two Bad Mice* by Beatrix Potter

CHAPTER 18

Fenimore stood blinking in the sudden glare. He had no right to do anything more. This was strictly a police matter. In his role as "family detective" he had no authority to touch or examine anything. He hovered in the doorway. As "family physician" he did have the authority to determine if Marie was alive or dead. Although he already knew the answer, he bent and felt for her pulse. None. He turned and noticed the shelf from which the bust had fallen. It hung loose, attached at only one end. The nails at the other end, tired of the weight of Hercules' bust (or whoever he was), had simply let go of the wall. The shelf, warped and stained, looked as if it had been with the house since it was built. But the nails, instead of bent and rusty—were straight and shiny, as if just brought home from the hardware store. (If he had been on the police force, he would have carefully removed one nail and pocketed it.) Instead he stared hard at the nail, committing its shape, size, and color to memory.

Turning back to the body, he fixed its angle permanently in his mind. He circled the room once looking for any obvious traces the murderer might have left behind. Finally his eyes came to rest on the piece of sculpture Marie had been working on. A male figure. The top half of the man emerged from blue-gray stone. He looked like a sailor, about to hoist a sail. His arms stretched upward as if hauling on some ropes and he wore the suggestion of a yachting cap.

He reminded Fenimore of someone.

"Doctor?" Mrs. Doyle called up the stairs. "Is everything all right?"

He flicked off the light, closed the door, and went to answer her.

When the police had left, the rest of the family members had been notified, and sedatives were administered to the two aunts, Fenimore took Mrs. Doyle into the library for a private word. She had almost required a sedative herself. She had taken complete blame for the tragedy.

"Oh, Doctor, I should have stayed with her. Or at least lured her downstairs—away from the studio. How could I have been so—?" She covered her face with her hands.

"Now, now." He patted her shoulder. "It wasn't your fault. That bust was set to fall on Marie sometime, whether you were there or not. But if you insist on blaming yourself—" His eye held a glint. "I know how you could make amends."

Mrs. Doyle glanced up, warily.

"How would you like to take a vacation at the seashore?"

"In December?"

"Mmm."

"But the office . . ."

"I can manage," he lied bravely.

"My clothes . . . ?"

"You and Judith are about the same size. I'm sure she could lend you some things to tide you over until I can bring your own things down."

"I'll need my wool slacks, two pairs of long johns, my flannel wrapper, my bedroom slippers, and . . ." She was rummaging in her pocketbook for her apartment key.

"Your bathing suit?"

She cast him a baleful glance. "What about my karate class?"

"I'll take care of that," he said blithely.

"You?" She surveyed him skeptically. Fenimore was not known for his athletic prowess. His attributes lay elsewhere.

"Not me, personally," he assured her. "I have a substitute in mind."

Mrs. Doyle tensed. "And who might that be?"

"Oh, an acquaintance," he said airily.

Mrs. Doyle's eyes narrowed. Fenimore turned away, pretending a fascination in an ancient map of Seacrest.

"You wouldn't!" She addressed the back of his neck. "You wouldn't wish that, that . . . on a bunch of defenseless, little old ladies." Her voice had risen an octave.

"Oh, so they're defenseless now. I thought they were hardy, agile—"

Mrs. Doyle glared.

"He told me he's well trained in the martial arts."

"A likely story—"

A light tap on the door. "Mrs. Doyle?" Judith.

"What's my excuse for staying?" whispered Mrs. Doyle anxiously.

"I need your help," Judith said in a louder voice.

Fenimore opened the door.

"It's time for Emily's bath, and with her poor hip it's really a two-person job. I used to ask Marie, but . . ."

Fenimore said. "She's all yours, Miss Pancoast."

Mrs. Doyle handed him her key. "Don't forget to water my violets," she said sternly.

Before she left the room, Fenimore whispered, "In between your nursing duties, keep your eyes and ears open for anything unusual and report back to me."

As he watched his capable nurse return to the parlor, his spirits rose. With Doyle on the scene—his occasional Watson—Fenimore's expectations for finding the murderer soared.

Before leaving Seacrest, Fenimore stopped at the inn. Although he had no desire for a Scotch, he ordered one. He had figured out who Marie's sailor was. He looked more at home pouring drinks than hauling sails.

"Hi, Doc! Hear there's been more trouble up the hill." Frank paused for enlightenment.

As Fenimore told him about Marie, he watched the bartender closely. He had been leaning with both hands on the bar. He sagged noticeably. From the shock of a personal loss—or merely a financial one? Marie had probably paid him handsomely for posing.

"She was working on a sculpture before she died. Was it you?" Fenimore asked.

"Yeah. She came in here one day and asked me to pose for her. With my clothes *on*, you understand." He actually blushed. "I was surprised to see her. She never comes in here. We were in high school together. Before she married Pancoast. But she never went high-hat. When we met in town she always had time for a chat. She even came to a class reunion once. Anyway, she said she had this idea about sculpting a sailor and she thought I had the right build." Again he reddened. "Well, since she's had all this trouble and everything, I didn't like to turn her down. So I said, 'What the hell, if the wife agrees.' It turned out she only needed me for a couple of sessions. Made a lot of sketches. But when it was time to go into stone, she explained, she wouldn't need me anymore. She wanted to pay me, but I wouldn't take anything. Then, just this afternoon, my wife calls and says Marie sent us a big Christmas basket—full of fruit and candy and cheese. Can you beat that? Her thinkin' of us— with all the trouble she has . . . had?" He brushed a quick hand across his eyes.

Fenimore concentrated on his Scotch.

"The Pancoasts are fine people," the bartender said finally.

"Yes, they are," Fenimore agreed. To himself, he added, "With one exception."

Fenimore made one more stop before heading back to Philadelphia. Whenever he came into Ben's Variety Store, he was overwhelmed by the number of objects stuffed into such a small cinder-block structure. Shelves stretched from floor to ceiling crammed with everything from kitchenware to office supplies, from hardware to cosmetics. With one quick look, Fenimore took in coffee grinders and frying pans, spiral notebooks and legal pads, wrenches and screwdrivers, face creams and nail polish. Whoever was in charge of the inventory was a genius. He suspected that Ben handled it himself.

A wholesome, dry goods smell permeated the place, reminding Fenimore of a store he had frequented in his youth. That store was long gone. He always tried to find an excuse to come to Ben's when he was in Seacrest. This time he had a ready-made excuse. Hearing Ben shuffling around in the darker storage regions, he squeezed his way between the crowded shelves to the back. He found him sorting screws.

Fenimore coughed.

Ben peered at him. "Oh, it's you."

"I'd like to see your nail collection."

"Over here." Ben led him through the murky gloom to the next aisle. Yanking a small flashlight from his belt, he played its beam over the nails.

Fenimore studied them carefully. Although the assortment was vast, none of them exactly resembled the one in Marie's studio. He frowned. "Is there any other store in Seacrest that sells nails?"

Ben snorted. "Dime store. Cheap stuff. Bend if you look at them. Made in Yugoslavia." He shut off the flashlight.

"Is it open?"

"Nope. Not 'til May first. When the tourists come."

"Well, thanks."

"Umph."

As Fenimore groped his way out, he wondered how Ben's customers ever found anything.

• • •

12/22 Mildred Pancoast's Diary:
Dear Diary,

   Marie is gone. And the killer didn't need a doll to set up this scene in the dollhouse. He (she?) used a clothespin. Poor Marie, reduced to a clothespin wearing an apron. If the killer can just use clothespins, there was no point burying the dolls. He can get clothespins anywhere. The house is full of them. And the hardware stores. Even the supermarkets. I'm not safe anymore, Diary. He can make a doll of me anytime. Tomorrow. Today. Maybe he's making one right now. Oh, God!

CHAPTER 19

Because of a fitful night, Fenimore overslept. When he came into the office Horatio was already there stuffing, stamping, and sealing the monthly bills.

"Why is everyone up so early?" Fenimore yawned.

"Not *everybody*." Horatio nodded at Sal. The cat lay on her back, four legs extended, as if she had died in her sleep and rigor mortis had set in. "And where's Doyle?" the boy asked, casting an accusatory glance at the empty desk that dominated the center of the room like a throne.

"*Mrs.* Doyle."

"I thought we were supposed to call all the broads 'Mzzzzzz' these days."

"Right. All except *Mrs.* Doyle."

"Huh."

"Mrs. Doyle will be out of town for an extended period. She's looking after a patient of mine in Seacrest."

Horatio frowned. "Who's gonna do all the work?"

"We'll manage. How's your mother?" Fenimore had followed Mrs. Lopez's case closely and made several house calls since his initial noctornal visit. (These subsequent calls had been made in the daytime, however.)

"Great. Whatever you did worked. She's starting to bug me again."

Fenimore bent to stroke Sal, who had risen from the dead to wrap herself around his left leg. When he unbent, he said, "I have a proposition for you."

Horatio looked up warily. Some of his employer's former propositions had ended in disaster.

"Didn't you mention that you were studying the martial arts?"

"Not *studying*. This guy knows a few moves and after school sometimes we go over to the yard and practice 'em."

"Would you care to demonstrate?"

"Here?" Horatio cast a disdainful eye around the cluttered office.

Fenimore opened the cellar door and with a broad sweep of his hand said, "Be my guest."

Always happy to stop working, Horatio obeyed.

The cellar was cool, clean, and welcoming, thanks to the recent yard sale—a perfect place to work out or demonstrate karate moves. After Horatio had shown Fenimore a few, the boy assumed a fighting stance. With a gleam in his dark eyes, he slid his left foot forward and raised his right knee, pointing it directly at Fenimore.

"Wait a minute," Fenimore stalled, feeling a surge of terror. "What's that called?"

"The Back Leg Roundhouse Kick."

Fenimore backed away.

With a grin, Horatio lowered his leg.

Fenimore's vision of himself lying prostrate on the cellar floor slowly receded.

As they made their way upstairs, Fenimore told Horatio's back, "You'll do."

"Do what?"

"As Mrs. Doyle's sub."

Horatio turned on the stair. "You want me to do all those fucking forms?"

"No, indeed." Fenimore's tone was solicitous. "I wouldn't dream of asking you to do forms." He shut the cellar door firmly. "I want you to teach her karate class."

It was Horatio's turn to wear a look of terror. "Those cackling broads?"

Fenimore nodded.

"You're crazy."

Fenimore had banked on this, and moved on. "See that?" He pointed to his microscope, its brass fixtures gleaming under the bell jar on his desk. It had belonged to his father, and to his grandfather before him. Fenimore had seen Horatio covertly admiring it. Once the boy had asked Fenimore to show him how it worked, but Fenimore had been too busy. "I found some old slides the other day. I'll give you some lessons."

Quick to recognize a bribe, Horatio said, "Forget it."

Fenimore pointed to the centrifuge next to it. Once he had caught Horatio playing with it. The boy had filled the tubes with water and set them spinning. "See, I didn't spill a drop,"

113

he had exclaimed when Fenimore came in. At the time, the doctor had not been amused, but now he said hopefully, "I'll teach you how to spin down urine samples."

"No way." Horatio continued energetically stuffing, stamping, and sealing.

Fenimore decided to drop the subject until he could come up with some better inducements. He settled into his favorite armchair to read the latest issue of *JAMA*. While he was absorbed in an article on cardiac transplants, an hour passed. When he looked up, Horatio had left for the day. The boy only worked until noon on Saturday. Fenimore was thinking seriously about lunch when the telephone rang.

"Could you throw in some electrocardiograms?" a familiar voice asked.

"What?"

"You know—along with the microscope and the centrifudge."

"Centrifuge."

"Whatever. Will you teach me to read them?"

"Do you know how long it took me to learn to read them?" Silence.

"Twelve years. More than two thirds of your lifetime. And I'm still learning."

"Nothing fancy. Just the basics."

"Just the basics." A sudden thought came to Fenimore. He could use someone to set up the electrocardiograph and prepare his patients for him. He had never been able to afford a technician. They were too expensive.

"Hurry up, for Chrissake! I'm using the dealer's phone and he's gettin' nervous."

Fenimore sighed deeply. "All right, Rat. It's a deal."

"But if any of those old broads hurt me," Horatio warned, "I'll sue."

"Don't worry. If any of those charming, elderly ladies harms a hair of your head, I'll—I'll send you to medical school." He laughed heartily.

When he was done laughing, the boy said quietly, "That's a deal."

CHAPTER 20

JANUARY

On New Year's Day Fenimore drove to Seacrest. He and Sal had spent a quiet evening at home. They had planned to stay up and watch the little ball descend in Times Square, but they had both fallen asleep before that thrilling moment. This morning, therefore, Fenimore was hangover-free. He hadn't warned the Pancoast sisters of his visit. He wanted to surprise them. To increase the surprise, he parked his car in the town and walked up the hill to their house. It was foggy and rainy. An unpromising way to start a new year. Lacking an umbrella, Fenimore turned up the collar of his raincoat and pulled down the brim of his hat. Water trickled down his neck and seeped into his shoes.

Squish, squish. Squish, squish.

Deciding to make his entrance from the rear of the house, he ducked behind a bush and slunk along the side wall to the garden.

What on earth are you trying to prove, Fenimore?

116

When desperate, one adopts desperate measures, he told himself.

He stood, the house at his back, looking out to sea. At least he was looking in that general direction. The fog blotted it out. But he could hear it. Something flickered out of the corner of his eye. He turned. The fog was so thick, the house was completely enshrouded. The only sounds were the steady drip of rain and the soft shush of the ocean.

Fenimore squished toward the bushes from which the movement had come. Swatting at the branches with his hat, he raised showers. He stood still, the rain falling on his bare head, listening.

A twig cracked.

He peered in the direction of the sound, but could see nothing. There were no more sounds. Feeling foolish, he moved toward the house. As he started up the steps, something brushed against his back. He spun. A figure running toward the side of the house. Fenimore was after him. Or—her? The figure he had glimpsed was thickly swathed in a long raincoat, a rain hat, and boots; there was no way to tell its sex or features. Fenimore increased his speed. When he reached the front of the house there was no sign of anyone. The fog was so thick he could barely make out the shaggy fir tree on the front lawn. It was hopeless. Whoever it was had got away.

Slowly, Fenimore returned to the rear of the house. When he tried the back door, it opened easily. Three murders had not convinced the Pancoasts to lock their back door. Shaking his head, he went inside.

The house felt empty. He had hoped, by the process of elimination, to find out who had been in the garden. The Pancoasts, if assembled inside, could not be the figure outside in the rain. But no one was inside. Where were they? He wandered through the dining room, the front hall, and into the parlor. No one. Rain and fog made the house darker than usual. Frugal people, the Pancoast sisters had left only one small lamp burning on the hall table.

Fenimore started to sit down on a needlepoint settee in the parlor, but, remembering his soggy condition, thought better of it. He wandered into the hall and looked at the dollhouse. It too was shrouded in darkness. The aunts had failed to leave a light burning in *its* hall. Even they forgot to play their little game sometimes. He peered closer. Maybe the answer to the mystery lay within these walls. He hunted for the light switch. While he was still hunting the small house burst into light.

Fenimore turned.

"It's over here." Adam stood a few feet away, his hand on a wall switch.

"I didn't hear you come in."

Adam glanced at his feet. "Sneakers."

"Where is everyone?"

"They're at our house. Susanne always has the family over on New Year's Day."

"And you?"

"I was there for a while. But I get fidgety. Like to keep busy. I came to fix the furnace. What are you doing here, anyway?" He looked at him quizzically. "Sleuthing?"

Fenimore, moderately embarrassed, said, "After a fashion."

"Be my guest. I'll be in the basement if you want anything."

Fenimore wandered out to the kitchen. On a chair by the door lay a damp windbreaker and a cap with a visor. Adam's outer garments. There was no sign of a long raincoat, a rain hat, or boots. Perhaps the mysterious figure had been a neighbor using the Pancoasts' garden as a shortcut to get out of the rain.

Fenimore made his soggy way back to the car.

CHAPTER 21

February

When the aunts decided not to hold their annual Valentine Tea, it wasn't Carrie, but Mrs. Beesley, the butcher's wife, who prevailed upon them. Mrs. Beesley was president of the Seacrest Senior Citizens' Society (SSCS) and every February she hired a bus to take the members to the tea.

"Oh, Miss Pancoast—"

Judith had answered the telephone.

"—the members will be so upset. Some of them have already made their valentines and they were so looking forward to exchanging them at the tea. I don't know what I'll tell them if you back out—"

Judith thought Mrs. Beesley's choice of words—unfortunate. She had never "backed out" of anything in her life (except her engagement, and that wasn't her fault).

"They've had their *hearts* set on it for weeks." Mrs. Beesley laughed at her feeble joke.

"Well, you know, Mrs. Beesley, we've had a bit of trouble here recently—"

"Oh, I know. It's terrible. The whole town's talking about it. Do they know who did it?"

Judith frowned into the receiver. "No," she said hastily, "but the police are working on it."

"Tch, tch. A terrible business." This remark was followed by an awkward silence.

"Well, let me talk to my sister about it and I'll let you know what we decide."

"Oh, thank you, Miss Pancoast." She found her voice again. "If you only knew how much this means—"

"Yes, yes, I know. Good-bye." It was Judith's turn to sigh as she replaced the receiver.

"But I thought we'd decided." Emily was vigorously polishing silver at the kitchen table with Mrs. Doyle. The Pancoasts were firm believers in industry as an antidote to disaster.

"I know. But I hate to disappoint people. Especially the elderly. They have so little to look forward to." Judith seemed oblivious to the fact that she and Emily fell into this category.

"Could I help?" asked Mrs. Doyle.

Emily looked at her. "Well—"

"Of course you can," Judith said. "You can greet them and show them the dollhouse. And we can ask Carrie to come do the refreshments. It's only from two to four. Oh, let's do it, Emily. It'll take our minds off—"

"What about decorations?"

"Oh, we have plenty left over from last year. Edgar and Adam can help."

"All right then. Go call her." Emily had already put down her polishing rag and was reaching for her walker so she could go hunt up some cardboard cupids and hearts.

Mrs. Beesley was ecstatic. The senior citizens were thrilled. Carrie was happy. And Mildred Pancoast was furious.

"How can you?" She confronted the aunts, hands on hips, eyes blazing.

"We just hated to disappoint—" mumbled Judith.

"We couldn't bear to see—" murmured Emily.

"It was an act of pure kindness, Mrs. Pancoast," put in Mrs. Doyle.

Mildred had spent a tedious morning cornering the clothespin market in Seacrest and she was not to be pacified. She had spent the previous day searching the aunts' house from top to bottom, confiscating all their clothespins (much to Judith's consternation—she hated dryers and loved the smell of clean sheets fresh from the line).

Adam had sat Mildred down and tried to talk some sense into her—scientist to scientist.

"It's not a case of cause and effect, Mildred," he had explained patiently. "The scenes in the dollhouse don't cause the deaths. . . ."

But she put her hands over her ears and hurried out of the room.

They were all worried about her.

Mrs. Doyle thought of recommending a good psychiatrist, but decided she had better consult Dr. Fenimore first.

Adam came through gallantly, putting up all the decorations in the big house. There were crimson hearts in every window and silver cupids in every corner. Strings of old-fashioned, lacy valentines were looped around mirrors, draped over mantels, and wound around banisters. A spray of red and white roses decorated the front door.

"If we're going to do it at all, we might as well do it right." Judith voiced her strong opinion.

But when it came to decorating the dollhouse, they balked. Too many sad memories lurked in those miniature rooms. In fact, the aunts tended to avoid the dollhouse these days. When they had to walk past it, they did so swiftly, averting their eyes.

Mrs. Doyle came to the rescue. "If you'll just show me what to do, I'll be glad to decorate it," she offered.

With relief, the aunts provided her with all the necessary materials and instructions and left her alone on the morning of the tea. As she began cutting out the tiny red hearts and pasting them in the windows, she remembered her own doll-house and the many happy weekends she had spent as a child playing with it. There had been no television back then. She had listened to the radio while she played. To *Grand Central Station, Let's Pretend,* and *The Green Hornet.*

Dr. Fenimore had told Mrs. Doyle which rooms had been the sites of the murder scenes and who had died where. In the dining room—Pamela. In the carriage house—Tom. In the studio—Marie. (Of course, Mrs. Doyle had been on hand for that one.) Fortunately, the carriage house and the studio didn't require decorating. Mrs. Doyle decided to start with the dining room and get it over with. She stuck a silver cupid in each corner of the mirror, found a vase of red and white carnations for the centerpiece, and decked the table with plates of tea sandwiches, sugar cakes, and heart-shaped cookies (all made from polymer). That was that.

It was time-consuming work because she had to be so careful not to break anything. Breakage had not been a problem with her own dollhouse. All the furniture had been molded from sturdy plastic (a new product right after the war). It had been much less nerve-racking arranging her tough purple bedstead, yellow refrigerator, and orange sofa, than moving this delicate Sheraton sideboard and those fragile Chippendale chairs. Also, her hands had been smaller then and more agile. Before arthritis had set in.

"It looks lovely, Mrs. Doyle."

The nurse looked up. "Oh, Carrie. Where did you come from?"

"I came early to set up. I have to go home and feed the kids at noon. Then I'll be back to serve at two. I hear you're staying on for a while."

The village grapevine. Dr. Fenimore had warned her about that. "Yes. I'm helping out until Miss Emily's hip is healed."

"It seems to be taking a long time." Carrie was interested in anything to do with healing.

"That's age, I'm afraid. Old bones take longer to mend."

"I've noticed that. When the kids break something, the cast comes off in a couple of weeks."

Mrs. Doyle straightened up with difficulty. She had been in a crouched position for over an hour and her knees and back were killing her. That had never happened to her when she had played with her own dollhouse.

"I'm up to Lesson Three—Muscles," Carrie said proudly.

124

"Good for you." Mrs. Doyle had instructed Dr. Fenimore to find the nursing course data in her apartment and mail it to Carrie. She had also taken it upon herself to go see the principal at the Seacrest High School and explain Carrie's situation. He had agreed to look into an introductory nursing course at a school nearby. "She's very bright," he reaffirmed what Mrs. Doyle already knew. He also promised to find child care for Carrie's younger brothers and sisters.

"Let me know when you get to Joints," Mrs. Doyle told Carrie. "Maybe you can do something for mine."

"I'd better get back to work," Carrie said. "See ya later, Mrs. Doyle."

Alone again, Mrs. Doyle began packing up the materials she hadn't used.

"They've put you to work, I see." Edgar stopped on his way to the kitchen. He was carrying a bag full of groceries. The aunts had sent him out for cream, extra sugar cubes, and some herb tea in case a senior citizen should request it. "Had quite a hunt for the herb tea," he said. "Seacrest doesn't go in for health foods in the winter. There's a store open here in the summer for the young vegetarians, but in the winter you don't get much call for herb teas or seaweed chips." His haggard face looked sadly incongruous above his perky red bow tie.

Mrs. Doyle grunted. "Ghastly stuff. Give me meat, butter, and eggs and an early grave. . . ." She stopped when she saw his expression. "I'm terribly sorry."

"No, no. My fault. Everything sets me off these days. That's why I keep busy. Better be getting these things out to the kitchen."

As she watched him make his way through the dining room, past the site of his daughter's recent death, Mrs. Doyle shook her head. How could one human being stand so much—the loss of a daughter, a son, and a wife—and still go on walking and talking? You go through the motions of living, she supposed—like a robot. Mercifully, the emotional centers became semi-paralyzed.

The front door flew open. Tad and Amanda rushed in, followed more slowly by Susanne and Adam.

"Hi, Mrs. Doyle. What are you up to?" Adam came over to examine her work. The children were already admiring it.

"Great job," Adam said. "The old folks will love it. Where are the aunts?"

"I think they're in the kitchen."

He made his way in that direction.

"Is my father here yet, Mrs. Doyle?" Susanne asked. The losses of the past few weeks had taken their toll on the young woman. Her face was thinner and her eyes and mouth were etched with new lines.

"Yes, he just passed through here on his way to the kitchen."

She hurried off in that direction.

The door opened again. In came Mildred wearing a fur coat and trailing a chartreuse wool scarf. But her feet and legs were dressed for summer—in sandals with no stockings. She didn't greet Mrs. Doyle, but sidled past her as if in a daze.

"Where are the children, Mrs. Pancoast?" Mrs. Doyle called after her.

She turned slowly, and with an effort focused on Mrs. Doyle. "What did you say?"

"Your children. Didn't you bring them?"

She seemed to mull this over, shook her head, and wandered into the dining room.

Mrs. Doyle followed her. Mildred pulled out a chair and sat down at the dining room table. "This was Pamela's place," she said.

"Yes, I know."

She grinned unexpectedly. "I hid all the clothespins."

"You did?"

"Where they'll never find them."

"Good for you."

"Now they'll never be able to make a doll of me."

"No indeed."

Suddenly she laid her head on the table.

Mrs. Doyle went into the library to place a call to Dr. Fenimore. It was more private there. As she dialed the number, she noticed a harpoon hanging over the mantel. A relic from the Pancoasts' whaling days. She remembered seeing one exactly like it over the mantel in the library of the dollhouse. Someone had cleverly fashioned it out of a safety pin.

"Doctor?"

"What's up?"

"Nothing," she said hastily. "At least nothing dreadful. I just wanted to tell you about Mildred. She's not herself. One minute she's having a temper tantrum and the next she's walking around in a daze, muttering incoherently. She spent the week collecting all the clothespins in Seacrest. Yesterday she ransacked the aunts' house for their clothespins and when she found them, she hid them."

"Hmm."

"I'm worried about her children. She has a baby, you know. When I asked her about them just now, she seemed very vague."

"You better check into that. Get someone to drive you over to her house—Susanne or Adam."

"Right."

"Anything else?"

"No, except—"

"Yes?"

"Well, I'm nervous about this party. Every time the Pancoasts give a party it seems to end in disaster. Thanksgiving, Christmas—now Valentine's. You can't come down, I suppose . . . ?" Mrs. Doyle trailed off.

"I wish I could, but I'm swamped. Working double duty, you know—without a nurse."

"How are my classes going?" She held her breath.

"Splendidly. Last night, Horatio took your pupils on a field trip."

She shook the receiver, afraid she had a bad connection.

"He planted each lady at a bus stop carefully chosen for its notorious reputation for muggings."

She gasped. "What happened?"

"Five muggers knocked silly, now cooling their heels in the lockup."

Mrs. Doyle smiled. "I told you, Doctor. Who says you can't teach old dogs new tricks?"

"I concede. But I don't think your lady friends would appreciate that appellation."

"Nonsense!" Mrs. Doyle snorted. "They'd take it as meant—as a compliment."

After Fenimore hung up, he sat staring at the telephone. Maybe Doyle was right. Maybe parties were a death knell for the Pancoasts. Maybe he should attend this one. He wasn't in a Valentine mood. Fenimore riffled through the mail. Medicare forms. Medical journals. Pharmaceutical ads. A postcard. On the front—a picture of a Parisian cemetery. He flipped it over. In Jennifer's hand he read:

Roses are red.
Violets are blue.
Paris is dead—
Without you.

He glanced at his watch. Only noon. If he hurried he could take care of his hospital patients and still make Seacrest in time for tea.

CHAPTER 22

After her talk with Fenimore, Mrs. Doyle went in search of Susanne or Adam. She found Susanne first—in the kitchen—helping the aunts make tea sandwiches.

"Of course," she responded to Mrs. Doyle's request. "We're almost finished here. I'll get my purse."

As soon as they were settled in the car, Susanne began to talk. She told the nurse how recent events were playing havoc with the family's nerves.

"Not just Mildred's," she said. "Adam's been terribly irritable, which is very unlike him. He snaps at the children and me. Yesterday he sent Tad to his room for next to nothing and when I tried to intervene, he walked out."

Mrs. Doyle clucked sympathetically. She was used to people confiding in her. They often told her the most intimate details of their personal lives on buses and trolleys. They had been doing this since she was in high school. She finally decided she had the kind of homely face that people thought they could trust. When she was younger, she would have gladly traded her face for a more beautiful one and put up with a little mistrust. But at fifty-eight, she had accepted it and tried to live up to the faith people placed in her.

"Adam's having trouble at school too—" Susanne took a turn a little too sharply. Mrs. Doyle grabbed the door handle.

"What sort of trouble?"

"Oh . . . the headmaster wants him to be easier on the boys. Not demand so much from them. Give them better grades for less work. It would make the school *look* better. But Adam has very high standards. He believes strongly in academic excellence. He thinks we're too soft as a country academically and that we're falling behind in the science race."

"Has he ever thought of teaching at a university?"

"Oh no. He feels that it's crucial to teach science at an early age—especially physics. If you wait too long—until they're in college—you'll lose some of the best minds."

"Hmm."

"He's very concerned that America is falling behind other countries—like Germany and Japan—in the sciences. Those countries have much stiffer science requirements. Teaching physics is almost a religion to Adam. A sort of—mission."

Mrs. Doyle was amazed to learn how much was seething beneath the surface of such a seemingly casual and relaxed young man. "Perhaps a vacation—" she suggested. "Does he have a spring break?"

"Yes. The boys get off for ten days in March. But Adam always spends his vacations on his boat."

"Boat?" Mrs. Doyle noticed they had left the town of Seacrest and were driving along the beach.

"Yes. He has a Lightning. A small craft. He stores it in the aunts' carriage house in winter. The boat has room for only two people and I'm rarely free to go with him because of the children. Here's Mildred's house." She drew to a stop in front of a spacious ranch house overlooking the beach.

A motherly, middle-aged woman answered their ring. She introduced herself as Mrs. Perkins. (A member of the generation that still believed in last names.) "Mrs. Pancoast asked me to stay till suppertime, because of the tea," she told them. "The baby's having his nap and the other children are in the playroom. Shall I get them?"

"No, that won't be necessary," Susanne said.

"Their mother seemed upset this morning," Mrs. Doyle explained. "We just wanted to make sure they were in good hands."

"And no wonder, what with all that's been going on!" Mrs. Perkins shook her head. "Poor things."

Mrs. Doyle caught a glimpse of toys scattered about and a couple of soda cans resting on good pieces of furniture. But the untidiness was no more than what one would expect in a house with young children.

They apologized for intruding and went back to the car. On the way home, Mrs. Doyle said, "Why don't you and your husband try to get away for a few days during spring break? You could leave your children with some kind soul like Mrs. Perkins. It would do you both good."

"That would be nice," Susanne murmured. "I'll try to persuade him. But you don't know what it's like to compete with a sailboat, Mrs. Doyle." She took her eyes off the road to send her a quick smile. "Competing with a beautiful, younger woman would be much easier."

Mrs. Doyle patted her shoulder. "It's worth a try."

CHAPTER 23

Mildred was spending the interlude between lunch and the Tea at a table by the window—her Tarot cards spread out before her. She seemed strangely serene. Not the dazed, anxious person of earlier that morning. Mrs. Doyle came and stood behind her. "Mind if I look?"

"Not at all." She continued to stare at the cards in silence.

Arranged in a semicircle, each card was decorated with a figure. The Emperor, the Fool, the Hermit—Mrs. Doyle read their captions to herself. They were brightly colored and resembled old paintings. "That's a funny one." She pointed to the figure of a man hanging upside down.

When Mildred looked up, her smile was mysterious. "Would you like a reading?"

"Oh, heavens no. I don't believe in that stuff."

"I feel good vibes coming from you, Mrs. Doyle. You have nothing to fear."

"I'm not *afraid*," she said huffily.

Mildred reached for a small chair and pulled it opposite her. "Have a seat."

Slowly, against her will, Mrs. Doyle sat.

"When I do a reading, I always like to start from scratch." Mildred drew the cards together, re-forming the pack. She took a small square of black silk from a wooden box at her elbow and wrapped the pack in it. The box was old and worn and looked handmade. She placed the wrapped cards in the box and closed the lid. "It's best to start fresh. I wouldn't want my wishes and desires to contaminate yours."

"Hogwash."

"That's what they all say in the beginning." Again that enigmatic smile. "These cards have an interesting history, Mrs. Doyle. Some people believe their symbols may be traced back to Egyptian times. Others date them from the early Renaissance—"

While Mildred talked, the cards were being cooked or cleansed in the mysterious wooden box, Mrs. Doyle assumed.

"The Major Arcana, or figure cards, represent archetypes which Jung says we all have in common in our collective unconscious. The Empress, for example, is the mother figure. And the Hermit is—"

"Mrs. Doyle! Don't tell me you've succumbed?" Judith stood in the doorway.

"Oh, mercy no, I was just—"

"She was just about to let me do a reading," Mildred said.

"Oh well, don't let me interrupt. I thought I'd go out on the porch for a breath of fresh air before the guests arrive."

Mildred waited until the front door closed behind Judith

before she reached into the box and retrieved the cards. Slowly she removed the black silk and asked Mrs. Doyle to shuffle the cards. When the nurse had finished, Mildred asked, "Do you have some overwhelming question? Something that has been dominating your thoughts recently?"

Yes, she thought. Who is the murderer? "Not really," she said.

"Then I will do the Whole Person Spread. This will give you an overall picture of yourself and help direct you toward the future path you should take."

"Back to Philly and my karate classes?"

Mildred smiled tolerantly.

Mrs. Doyle tried to say "Hogwash" again, but somehow the word stuck in her throat. Instead she concentrated on the pretty pictures Mildred was laying on the table. There were four of them, in red and yellow, black and gold, The Magician, the Hermit, the Wheel of Fortune, and . . . Death.

Mrs. Doyle made an involuntary movement.

"No," Mildred said quickly. "Death doesn't mean the end in this context. It means transition—a new beginning. The beginning of a new life, perhaps."

"I like my old life," Mrs. Doyle said querulously.

"These changes may not refer to time or place—but to the spirit," Mildred assured her. "You may be about to move to a higher spiritual plane."

Suddenly a familiar face flashed before Mrs. Doyle—Father Clancey's. Followed by a familiar voice with just a touch of an Irish brogue. "Testing the waters, Kathleen?" it said.

She let Mildred finish her reading, but she had lost interest. In the nick of time, she had been pulled back from the abyss.

CHAPTER 24

Mrs. Beesley led the parade of senior citizens up the path to the Pancoasts' front door. Many of the ladies favored red pantsuits for the occasion. Many of the gentlemen sported red neckties. They all wore the same expressions of eager anticipation.

"I'm so glad we didn't disappoint them," Judith said.

"Yes, it would have been a pity," Emily agreed.

When the doorbell rang, they both went to answer it. Emily wielded her walker with the same exuberance as she had wielded her hockey stick as a girl.

Mrs. Doyle was the designated dollhouse guide. She guarded it like a sentry and fielded questions like a veteran museum docent. The aunts had primed her with answers to the most frequently asked questions, such as, "Is the chandelier real crystal?" and "Do the toilets flush?" The answer to both was—"No." But she wasn't prepared for the shrewd heavyset woman in a pink pantsuit, who asked, "Where did the murders take place?"

"Uh—" Mrs. Doyle hesitated. Then, deciding on a straightforward approach, she pointed, in quick succession, to the dining room, the carriage house, and the studio. But she underestimated her audience.

"You missed one. Who's that in the library?" Pink pants said.

"Probably a Pancoast who overdid the booze," hooted an old codger who fancied himself the life of the party. "These displays are very realistic, you know." He guffawed.

"Oh, Harry," squealed a petite, blue-haired lady who was hanging onto his arm. The other women tittered.

Mrs. Doyle bent to look in the library. Lying in the middle of the miniature oriental rug was a clothespin. Tucked between its splayed halves was the harpoon which had recently hung over the mantel. Adorning the neck of the clothespin was a tiny red bow tie.

Dimly, Mrs. Doyle was aware of the doorbell. From a long distance, she heard Judith greet someone. Elderly faces tilted toward her—wearing inquiring expressions. She felt behind her for the banister to steady herself.

"I don't know who that is," she managed to say. "Tea is being served in the dining room. Won't you go in, please?"

Always ready for refreshments—a change from their boring institutional diet—the senior citizens followed her suggestion and moved in a body toward the dining room.

"Mrs. Doyle! Look who's here!" Judith was approaching with someone in tow.

When she saw who it was, Mrs. Doyle almost fell on his neck. She restrained herself with difficulty.

"What's wrong?" Fenimore asked sharply, although her face told him all.

"Nothing. Just a bit tired. Think I'll sit down." She promptly sat on the bottom step of the staircase.

"Judith, would you get my nurse a cup of tea? She looks a bit fagged."

"Oh, dear Doctor, I'm afraid we've worn her out. She's been working since dawn. Stay right there, Mrs. Doyle. Don't move. I'll be right back. Oh, dear—" And Judith scurried off like the White Rabbit.

"Now," said Fenimore.

"In the library. Look!" she commanded.

He drew a quick breath. "The other library. Where—?"

"Over there." Mrs. Doyle pointed to a door down the hall, next to the parlor.

"Try to detain the guests in the dining room, Doyle," he said, over his shoulder.

As Fenimore placed his hand on the doorknob, he felt a wave of déjà vu. How many more times would he have to go through this? Turning the knob, he went inside.

"Was that Dr. Fenimore I saw just now?" Mildred confronted Mrs. Doyle by the sideboard.

Mrs. Doyle's usual flair for repartee deserted her. She nodded.

"I want to speak to him. I want to know why he hasn't made more progress in his investigations. It's been months. I thought I saw him go in the library—" She started off.

"Mrs. Pancoast!"

She turned.

Mrs. Doyle forced a smile. "I think he's in the 'men's'."

"Oh, all right. But let me know as soon as he comes out."

Her former dazed attitude had been replaced by a belligerent one.

It was Mrs. Doyle who felt dazed. She watched the guests gobbling their sandwiches and guzzling their tea as if through a thick fog. All the time she was watching them, her mind was in the library.

"Everything seems to be going well." Emily brought her walker to rest beside Mrs. Doyle.

"Yes." Mrs. Doyle pulled herself together. "They all seem to be enjoying themselves."

"Judith told me we've exhausted you. We certainly appreciated your help, Mrs. Doyle. I hope you won't be too anxious to leave us."

"I'll stay as long as you need me," she said graciously.

"In that case, I must try to delay my recovery." Emily smiled and moved off.

"Have you seen my father, Mrs. Doyle?" Susanne came up to her. "I seem to be always losing him."

"No, I haven't," she said shortly. Then, in an attempt to make amends, she added, "The aunts may have sent him on an errand."

"Or . . . maybe he's in the library." Susanne turned toward the hall.

"Wait!" Mrs. Doyle took her arm and drew her over to the table. "Why don't you have some tea first. You look a little peaked. It'll perk you up."

"Oh, I don't know—"

"Here, I'll pour some for you." Mrs. Doyle poured her a full cup and escorted her to a chair next to a very loquacious senior citizen she had noticed earlier. She counted on Susanne's good manners to keep her beside him for at least a quarter of an hour. She glanced at her watch.

"Caught you!" Mrs. Beesley pounced on Mrs. Doyle. "Clock-watching, weren't you? Now don't worry. I promised to get you all home in time for supper." To prove her statement, she began prodding the others toward the parlor. "Come now, everybody. Time to exchange your valentines."

Good heavens! Mrs. Beesley had mistaken *her*, Kathleen Doyle—a young fifty-eight-year-old—for one of her senior citizens! Surely, Seacrest hadn't aged her that much? She scanned her reflection in the mirror over the sideboard.

It had.

Slowly she made her way out of the dining room in search of Dr. Fenimore. She found him emerging from the library. He too had aged.

"Edgar?"

"Yes. With the harpoon." He scanned the hall. "Where is Susanne?"

"In there." Mrs. Doyle pointed to the dining room

"I must tell her, before I call the police."

"She's been looking everywhere for him."

"I've really botched this, Doyle." His face wore a look of anguish she had never seen before. "What about you? Have you uncovered anything?"

She shook her head. "They all seem such nice, normal people. Except Mildred. But she's just a . . . nut."

"Whoever is behind this—" His tone was menacing.

Sporadic giggles and gruff guffaws emanated from the parlor. The senior citizens were enjoying their valentines.

Fenimore straightened his shoulders and went to find Susanne.

CHAPTER 25

When Fenimore stepped into his office he sniffed. Perfume? And something else was different. Of course Mrs. Doyle's bulky presence was missing. But there was no sign of Horatio, either. In his place, crouched over his filing cabinet, was a scantily clad female figure. She looked up.

"How do you do?" Fenimore said.

"Oh, you must be the doctor." She pushed a strand of hair from her eyes and stared.

"I don't believe I've had the pleasure. . . ."

She giggled. "Tracy Sparks. The new temp."

Mrs. Doyle had mentioned something about hiring temporary help in her absence, but this was the first one he'd seen.

"Hey, Doc." Horatio ambled in from the kitchen, munching an apple. He tossed another to Ms. Sparks. "For after work," he said, sternly.

She quickly bent to her filing.

Sal appeared from one of her hiding places. Fenimore picked

her up, glad to find something familiar in his office.

"What about my lessons?" Horatio asked, without preamble.

Fenimore started visibly. With all the uproar over the Pancoast case, not to mention caring for his other patients, he had completely forgotten about his promise to Horatio. Despite his exhaustion, he said, "Now would be a good time."

Since the Pancoasts were foremost in his mind, he decided to explain Emily's heart condition. He drew out her file. "Miss Pancoast suffers from a condition called the Sick Sinus Syndrome."

"I thought we were gonna talk about her heart."

Fenimore looked at him.

"Aren't the sinuses in the nose? My uncle's always complaining about his. He has terrible headaches and snorts a lot."

It was going to be a long evening. "This is a different kind of sinus. The word 'sinus' means a cavity or hollow. They can be found in many parts of the body. The one I was referring to is a hollow in the chamber of the heart that collects blue blood. This is where the natural pacemaker of the heart is located. It's called the 'sinus node.' "

Horatio was paying attention.

"The heart rate varies according to the size of each creature. The larger the creature the slower the heart rate. The whale's heart beats twelve times a minute, a hummingbird's—six hundred and fifteen. A normal adult human heart beats anywhere from sixty to one hundred times a minute." Fenimore pulled his stethoscope from his pocket and handed it to Horatio. "Put those in your ears."

He obeyed.

Fenimore started to push up Horatio's T-shirt. The boy yanked it off and tossed it in a corner. When Fenimore planted the silver disk on his chest, Horatio jumped. "It's cold!" he yelped.

"That's what they all say." Fenimore massaged the disk with his hand to warm it and placed it back on the boy's chest a little to left of center. He looked at his watch. When the second hand reached twelve, he told Horatio to start counting.

"One, two—" he began under his breath.

When the second hand had completed one rotation, Fenimore said, "Stop! How high did you get?"

"Seventy."

"Good. I'm happy to inform you that you are a healthy fifteen-year-old. Cardiac-wise, that is," he modified.

Horatio grinned.

"Now, Emily's heart"—he took an electrocardiogram from her file—"beats at a rate of sixty-two a minute, a normal rate. But there's one problem. Every now and then it slows down— and even stops."

Horatio blinked.

"Yes. That's not good. And the reason it stops is because her sinus node isn't working well. The sinus node produces the electrical impulse that causes the heart to contract and push the blood around the body. When it isn't working, the blood stops moving around."

"And she gets dizzy cause her brain's not gettin' enough blood."

"Right." Fenimore beamed, pleased that his pupil had remembered so much. "But today we have a way to correct this."

145

He fumbled in his drawer and came up with an oblong, shiny metal object about the size of a cigarette lighter.

"A pacemaker," said Horatio.

"You've seen one?"

"He nodded. On *S&I—Science & Invention*—a TV show."

Hmm. Fenimore made a mental note to watch more TV. He tossed the pacemaker at Horatio. Two long wires protruded from one end. He fiddled with them.

"One wire is embedded in the collecting chamber, the other in a pumping chamber," Fenimore said.

The temp was hovering in the doorway.

Fenimore looked up with a frown. He hated to be interrupted. "Yes?"

"My question's for Mr. Lopez," she drawled. If she hadn't batted her ample eyelashes in Horatio's direction, Fenimore would have wondered whom she was talking about.

"I'll be with you in a minute," Horatio dismissed her with a curt nod.

To Fenimore's amazement, Ms. Spark's gaze lingered over Horatio's bare chest a little longer than necessary. He observed his part-time help with new eyes.

Fenimore reached behind him and pulled down a wall chart. The chart revealed a detailed diagram of the heart. He pointed out the collecting chamber and the pumping chamber.

"Once the pacemaker is implanted, when Emily's sinus node fails to produce its electrical charge, the man-made pacemaker senses this and supplies a charge of its own. It keeps doing this until Emily's sinus node begins to work again."

"Wow!"

"Yes. It is a kind of miracle." Warmed by his pupil's enthusiasm, Fenimore sorted through Emily's electrocardiograms and took out three of them. "The first shows her heartbeat when her own sinus node is working; the second shows when it isn't working well; the third shows when the pacemaker kicks in and takes over."

Emily Pancoast's Electrocardiograms

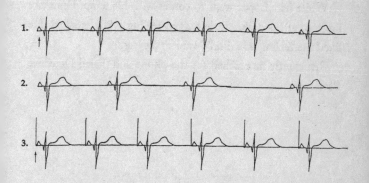

1. Emily's natural pacemaker (arrow) is functioning; her heart beats at 60 a minute.
2. Emily's natural pacemaker slows; she becomes dizzy.
3. The artificial pacemaker kicks in (arrow) and restores Emily's normal heart rate.

"But where does the pacemaker get its electricity? There's no plug."

"A battery. There's a battery inside the pacemaker."

"But doesn't it give out? I have to buy new ones for my boom box all the time."

"Absolutely." He grinned at his bright pupil. "That's why we hitch Emily up to that transmitter you saw down at Seacrest.

They check it every three months to make sure her battery hasn't run down. It has to be replaced about every five years. But it's a minor operation, done on an outpatient basis. She's home the same day."

"Huh."

"Is that all you have to say?" He slipped the electrocardiograms back in the folder.

"Cool, man." Horatio rose and stretched.

"That's better."

While Mr. Lopez went to confer with his temp, Fenimore lingered at his desk a little longer, feeling oddly satisfied. He liked the feeling. He didn't want to let it go.

Reluctantly he reached for the phone and dialed Detective Rafferty's number.

CHAPTER 26

They were well into their martinis before Fenimore outlined the Pancoast affair to his friend. He was not proud of the part he had played in it so far.

Rafferty looked stern. "I warned you about this amateur dabbling, Fenimore. You'd better leave it to the police."

"The Seacrest Police have come up with zilch. Now, there are rumors that the state police have been called in. I was only trying to help my friends," Fenimore protested.

"What would you think if I started dabbling in medicine? Dispensing pills to *my* friends?"

"That's different," Fenimore grunted.

"What you're doing is just as dangerous. And just as illegal, I might add." The policeman polished off his martini.

"Are you going to turn me in?"

Rafferty stared, then grinned. "No. But I seriously warn you off. Have another?"

Over their second martini, Rafferty mellowed and ceased reprimanding his friend. Fenimore ventured a question. "Any thoughts on the case?"

"Has it occurred to you that you're too close to these 'aunts'—these old patients of yours—to evaluate them objectively?"

"But—" Fenimore started to object.

"Be honest," Rafferty stopped him. "Haven't you eliminated them from your list of possible suspects?"

Fenimore stirred uneasily.

"Just as I thought." Rafferty reached for the menu. "You're too emotionally involved in this case."

Fenimore waited while his friend decided between pork chops and steak. "But they're both elderly. And one, at least, is in frail health."

"Too frail to put poison in a piece of pumpkin pie? Too frail to turn a key in an ignition and shut a garage door? Too frail to hammer a few nails into a small shelf . . . ?"

"Too frail to wield a heavy harpoon," Fenimore parried.

"Just how heavy is a harpoon?" Rafferty countered.

Fenimore shrugged.

"Did you lift it?"

"Of course not. There might have been prints . . ."

"A harpoon is not much heavier than a large arrow. It's built to fly through the air. Anyone of average strength could manage it."

Fenimore thought of the Red Umbrella Brigade and Doyle's agile octogenarians. He placed his order for bluefish stuffed with crabmeat. When the waiter left them, he said, "But the murderer knocked him out before wielding that harpoon. The medical examiner found a bump on the back of his head. How could my elderly patient have managed that?"

"The *back* of the head. The murderer came at him from behind. There was no struggle. He never knew what hit him."

Fenimore mulled over Rafferty's words. Emily—a murderess? Ridiculous. Judith? Inconceivable. What about Mildred or Adam? Unlikely. Then there was Susanne. Could she have done in her mother, father, sister, brother? Absurd. Frank, the bartender? He had been tending bar on Thanksgiving Day before a host of witnesses. Lastly, reluctantly, he remembered Carrie. Preposterous. All preposterous. What could possibly be their motives?

As if reading his mind, Rafferty said, "Have you come up with a motive?"

Fenimore shook his head.

"There are only a few, you know. Money. Love. Power. Revenge. Or a combination."

Rafferty had given Fenimore enough to chew on. He turned the conversation away from the Pancoasts, to the Phillies. The two men had a love-hate relationship with that ill-fated team. Although, at bottom, Fenimore was an ardent fan, he couldn't resist needling his friend when the team entered its perennial losing streak. "How does the lineup look this year?" he asked.

"Good. Expect a better than average season." Rafferty glanced up warily, waiting for one of Fenimore's usual putdowns.

None was forthcoming. Fenimore was too preoccupied tonight to indulge in his ritual teasing.

• • •

The meeting with Rafferty had been productive. The next morning, despite a mild hangover, Fenimore was hot on the trail of motives. After receiving permission from Emily and Judith to examine their finances, he placed a call to the First National Bank of Seacrest. Judith had alerted the appropriate trust officer to his call, and after he provided the necessary identification, a bank officer told him how the Pancoast assets were held. At present they were held equally by Emily, Judith, and their recently deceased brother—Edgar—in the form of stocks, treasury bonds, mutual funds, and real estate.

Fenimore then called the family lawyer, who had also been alerted, and learned how these assets were to be allocated in the event of the death of any of them.

1. Emily's would go to Judith.
2. Judith's—to Emily.
3. Edgar's—now that Pamela, Tom, and Marie were deceased—would be divided equally among his remaining heirs—Susanne, his son's wife Mildred, and their children. (Fenimore refused to let himself think about the children.)

So much for money. On to love.

Fenimore's only source for knowledge of the heart was the infamous Seacrest grapevine. He decided that Mrs. Doyle was in a better position to research that. He called her.

"But Doctor, the aunts are too old for love!"

"Nonsense. If your octogenarians are young enough for karate, the aunts are young enough for love."

"But who—?"

"That's for you to find out, Doyle. Keep your ear to that grapevine. The best grapes are probably Mrs. Beesley, the butcher's wife, Frank, the bartender, and Carrie."

"Oh, Doctor, I couldn't go into a bar alone."

"Come, come, Doyle. You're behind the times. Haven't you heard of women's liberation? You're free to go anywhere, anytime—without fear of social condemnation."

Mrs. Doyle gave one of her famous snorts—the one especially reserved for her employer's judgment.

"Oh, and, Doyle . . ." he went on, ignoring her rude noise, "keep your ears open for any references to power or revenge—the other two possible motives."

"Oh, right." Mrs. Doyle could no longer hide her exasperation. "Mrs. Beesley is going to tell me that Edgar confided in her one day, while she wrapped up his pork chops, that he harbored a deep desire for her, but Mr. Beesley and Marie prevented him from consummating it. And," without pausing for breath, "Carrie is going to confess that when she was babysitting for Susanne one day, the children informed her that their mother hadn't gone out at all, but was upstairs entertaining Frank, the bartender, in her bedroom. And Frank will regale me with an account of Mildred's wild passion for Adam, who she pretends to hate. She revealed this to him over a few gin and tonics one night. Emily, of course, will confess during afternoon tea that she was in love with Judith's seaman fiancé before Judith ever thought of him, and when he transferred his affections to her sister, she was overcome with jealousy and rage. Judith, on the other hand, blames Emily for revealing the secret of their planned elopement to her father, and has silently born a grudge for sixty years. . . ."

"That's the ticket, Doyle. You've got the hang of it. Now get cracking. I'm counting on you." He hung up—cutting off another offensive snort.

CHAPTER 27

It was after the rector had performed the little graveside ceremony over Edgar Pancoast's remains that Mildred came up with the idea of burning the dollhouse.

"But Mildred, what good would that do?" asked Emily.

Her eyes glittered. Dressed in black, except for a cape traversed by a single, diagonal slash of emerald green, she said, "If the house is gone, these ghastly murders will end."

"I thought I explained," Adam began wearily. "The house has nothing to do with it."

"How little you scientists know. There's a whole world out there—teeming with spirits and auras and forces—you know nothing about."

"And by avoiding black cats, stepladders, Friday the thirteenth—and burning down dollhouses, you keep them at bay?" He stared at her.

She narrowed her eyes and uttered an expletive that shocked even Mrs. Doyle. The aunts pretended not to hear. Despite all the tragedies, they still could not bear the thought of destroying the dollhouse. Adam turned away.

Dr. Fenimore had been unable to attend Edgar's services because of an emergency in Philadelphia. But he had called Mrs. Doyle and instructed her to observe the Pancoasts carefully—before, during, and after the service. "People tend to let down their defenses during times of stress," he said.

"Thanks for the psychology lesson," she said.

Mrs. Doyle was doing her best as house psychologist now. She had planted herself on the love seat in the center of the parlor, from which vantage point she could see and hear everyone. But all she had determined thus far was—everyone's nerves were frayed to the breaking point. They were snapping at each other like a bunch of starving alligators.

Susanne was the only one not taking part. Isolated by the magnitude of her grief, she sat to one side, staring out the window at the bare winter garden. Adam came and sat beside her, placing his hand over hers.

Mrs. Doyle turned to look at Mildred. She was pacing restlessly, now and then picking up a knickknack and blowing off some invisible dust. Finally she threw herself down on the love seat beside Mrs. Doyle. "I don't know why they won't listen to me," she muttered, still clutching a pink-cheeked shepherdess.

"It's because they're upset," Mrs. Doyle said soothingly. "They can't think straight."

"Then you agree with me?" She looked at her.

"Well, I—"

"You do, don't you? You see the connection. If the house is gone, the murders will stop."

Sensing that the woman was verging on hysteria, Mrs. Doyle picked her words carefully. "Let's say, I think the murderer is a compulsive, methodical person, and he or she has set up this pattern of arranging a duplicate of each murder in miniature before committing the real murder. And he or she probably wouldn't commit another murder without first setting up such a scene, but—"

"You do see!" The glitter was back. "Adam! Everyone. Mrs. Doyle agrees with me. She thinks we should burn the doll-house."

"Wait—even if the dollhouse is gone, the murderer still has his or her reason to kill."

Everyone's eyes were on Mrs. Doyle.

"But you said the murderer was very methodical and wouldn't commit a murder without first creating a scene in the dollhouse. Those were your very words," Mildred confronted her.

The aunts looked distressed.

Adam shrugged.

Susanne continued to stare out the window.

"If you feel it's best, Mrs. Doyle—" Emily spoke hesitatingly.

"Yes, of course. We'll do anything—" Judith was too overcome to finish.

"I only thought that maybe if we upset the murderer's pattern—" Mrs. Doyle felt she was out of her depth. What would the doctor say?

"Well, when shall we do it, Emily?" said Judith.

"The sooner the better, I suppose," Emily said.

Adam left the room.

Mildred smiled the smile of the victor.

Mrs. Doyle, the psychologist, remained rooted to the love seat, staring abashedly at her feet.

. . . they put it into the red hot crinkly paper fire . . .

—*The Tale of Two Bad Mice* by Beatrix Potter

CHAPTER 28

MARCH

The dollhouse burning was delayed. It was a simple matter of logistics. It was too heavy and too cumbersome for the aunts to move, even with Mrs. Doyle's help. Edgar, of course, was no longer available. And Adam refused to have anything to do with the project. Mildred had come up with her own solution. She had offered to chop it up in the hallway and carry the pieces to the backyard for burning. But the aunts had steadfastly refused her offer. It was one thing to burn their prize possession. There was something clean and sacred about fire. But to wantonly hack and chop . . . It was unthinkable. So it remained in its place of honor on the platform in the front hall, until someone could come up with a solution for removing it.

Meanwhile, the Pancoasts continued to go through the motions of living—keeping as busy as possible. It was March. Winter was on the wane. And the town of Seacrest was remembering that it was a summer resort. Everywhere, there were signs of preparation for the great onslaught of vacation people who would begin to arrive on Memorial Day. Shop owners were decorating their shop windows. Trucks were unloading goods of every description out front. Everything from cartons of suntan lotion to bales of T-shirts with "Seacrest" (or "Sexcrest") emblazoned on them in fluorescent pink or orange.

When Mrs. Doyle went to do her weekly shopping, she noticed that the town had lost its dour, dead-of-winter appearance and had taken on a more cheerful aspect. Gone was the brown canvas that had covered the pavilion on the boardwalk to protect it from battering winter winds and corroding salt spray. Someone was energetically painting its roof a bright emerald green. The benches along the boardwalk were also receiving new coats of paint. And when she cast her eye toward the ocean, she saw several colorful sails bouncing on the choppy waves. A few enterprising sailors were actually braving the March winds.

Later, as Mrs. Doyle let herself into the house, loaded with bags of groceries, she felt exhilarated. Although her hands and feet were numb with cold, the glimpse she had had of a town renewing itself had warmed her spirits. She burst into the kitchen full of good feeling.

Emily and Judith were seated at the kitchen table, grimly staring at each other. They barely acknowledged her entrance.

"What's wrong?"

Emily pressed her hands to her eyes. Judith twisted her rings and looked away.

Mrs. Doyle put down her groceries with a thud. "Tell me."

Judith took a deep breath. "Susanne was just here."

"And?"

"Adam went sailing this morning and he hasn't come back."

"Well—it's still light."

"He promised to be back at three. He was supposed to pick up the children at the movies." Judith said.

"And he never came?"

"No. They waited and waited. They didn't have enough money to call home. They'd spent it all on candy and popcorn. Finally they walked home. Susanne was frantic. She came up here looking for them. While she was here, the sitter called and said they had come home."

"The sitter was there," Emily explained, "because Susanne and Adam had planned to go away for a few days. The car was all packed—"

So Susanne had taken Mrs. Doyle's advice. "And he still isn't back?" she said.

"No," Judith said. "And that isn't all—" She gave her rings a violent twist.

"The sailboat is missing from the dollhouse carriage house," said Emily.

Mrs. Doyle thought of the colorful sails bobbing on the water. How cheerful they had looked. Heavily, she let herself down on the nearest kitchen chair. "Maybe one of the children took the boat to play with—" she murmured without conviction.

The doorbell.

"They're here," Judith looked at Emily.

"I'll go," said Mrs. Doyle. She went to the door, expecting

to find Susanne and the children. Instead, she found two strange, husky men standing on the doorstep.

"Sunflower Movers," said the taller one.

"Oh, you must have the wrong house. No one is moving here."

"Yes, we are," Emily called out. "Tell them to come in, Mrs. Doyle."

Mrs. Doyle stepped aside. The two men came into the hall.

"Where is it?" one asked.

"Over there." Judith pointed to the dollhouse.

They looked puzzled. "But it's still full of stuff."

"That goes too." Emily joined them, her cane tapping lightly on the polished floor.

The man shrugged, looked at his partner, and back to Judith. "Where do you want it?"

"In the backyard—a good fifty feet from the house," Judith said.

"Okay, ma'am. Whatever you say." He took hold of one side of the dollhouse. His partner grabbed the other. In a matter of seconds they had transported the cumbersome structure—as if it were made of toothpicks—through the dining room, the kitchen, the pantry, and deep into the backyard. They set it down gently, hardly disturbing its fragile contents, and looked to the aunts for further instructions.

"That will be all, thank you," Judith said.

The shorter man scratched his head and looked around. "Won't it get wet out here?"

"We've thought of that—" Judith began.

"Everything's taken care of," Emily said.

When they were back in the hallway, Emily asked how much they owed them.

The taller mover, who was the spokesman, frowned. "Let's see. It's after hours. I'll have to charge you overtime. Then there was the trip up here. But it was a small job. Twenty-five should cover it."

Emily drew a small needlepoint wallet from her pocket and carefully counted out the bills.

"Don't you want a receipt?" He had pad and pen ready.

"That won't be necessary."

As soon as the door closed, Emily turned to her sister. "Do you have the matches?"

Judith handed her the box.

Mrs. Doyle followed the two elderly ladies out the back door into the garden. A few crocuses were up and some snowdrops. Judith plucked a handful of straw from a flower bed and quickly stuffed some into each of the small rooms. The wind, which had caused the choppy waves on the ocean earlier, had died down. Emily had no trouble lighting the match.

She touched it first to a curtain in the bedroom. The flame quivered, leapt, and spread. The towers, turrets, and balconies toppled first. Then the cupola on the carriage house and the porch with the gingerbread. One more bright, brief flare—a crackling sound—and all that was left was a pile of red embers and the smell of burnt plywood mixed with glue.

The two ladies waited in the garden until the embers turned to gray. Then, arm in arm, they walked slowly back to the house.

Mrs. Doyle followed at a respectful distance.

3/22 Mildred Pancoast's Diary:
Dear Diary,

They finally did it. The old birds took my advice and burned the damned dollhouse to the ground. Now maybe we'll have some peace!

CHAPTER 29

Adam's Lightning was found washed up on the beach a few days after his disappearance. Upon examination, the police discovered that the ropes which held the mainsail had been deliberately tampered with. They had been weakened by shaving with a knife so that they broke as soon as the sail was struck by the first hard gust of wind. There had been plenty of hard gusts the day he had taken his boat out.

Dr. Fenimore came down immediately. (Indeed, he was becoming a regular commuter.) He placed Susanne under sedation and asked Mrs. Doyle to arrange for someone to take care of her children. Mildred offered to keep them, but Mrs. Doyle thought she was too unstable for any additional responsibilities. The kindly and capable Mrs. Perkins was chosen instead.

Fenimore sequestered himself with the Seacrest Police for an hour. He was informed that the state police had been called in and were officially working on the case. Later, in the company of a state policeman, Fenimore was allowed to examine

Adam's boat—and the defective ropes. It was agreed that if Adam had fallen overboard, the water temperature that day (thirty degrees) would have prevented him from swimming more than a short distance without freezing, and he would have—ultimately—drowned. They had searched for eyewitnesses among the few hardy fishermen and sailors who had ventured out that day. But they could locate only one other sailor who actually remembered seeing Adam set out. It had been early, around 7 A.M. But he had lost track of him soon afterward. Sailing his own boat had required all his attention. It had been that kind of day.

After his consultation with the police, Fenimore came back to the Pancoast house to get a firsthand story of Adam's disappearance from the aunts. When he entered the front hall he was struck by the yawning chasm at the bottom of the staircase. Mrs. Doyle gave a quick, whispered account of the fate of the dollhouse.

He shook his head. "And the contents."

"All gone. Up in smoke."

He chastised himself for lamenting such a trivial loss, compared with the loss of Adam and the others. But he couldn't help feeling angry at such pointless destruction, and blamed Mildred for it.

Mrs. Doyle was careful not to reveal her part in Mildred's plan—or her own halfhearted acquiescence to it. She still wondered at herself. Had she really believed all that stuff about "breaking the murderer's pattern"? Or, like Mildred, was she becoming superstitious in her old age?

The aunts insisted on giving Fenimore a light supper before

he returned to Philadelphia. It was a quiet meal. Carefully skirting the subject which was foremost on their minds, they made desultory conversation about the weather, the food, and their respective states of health. Emily complained of headaches; Judith of arthritis, and Mrs. Doyle—of chronic indigestion. The doctor diagnosed "nerves" in every case and recommended exercise in the form of brisk walks. Except for Emily. Although her hip was healing nicely, brisk walks were still out of the question. For her, the doctor prescribed aspirin.

During dessert, in an attempt to divert them, Fenimore told them about the house calls he had made on Horatio's mother.

"How can people live in such a place?" murmured Emily, when he had finished.

"Maybe we could find them something better," said Mrs. Doyle. "I think there was a vacancy in my apartment building—"

Fenimore was touched. He knew what a sacrifice it would be for Doyle not only to share her workplace with Horatio, but also her living quarters. He said only, "How would they pay for it?"

"Perhaps we could help," Judith offered.

Fenimore shook his head vehemently.

"Why not?" asked Mrs. Doyle.

"Because Horatio and his mother, and probably all the rest of the family, suffer from a rare and incurable disease."

"Oh no," gasped the two sisters.

But Mrs. Doyle was suspicious. She had never known her employer to betray a patient's confidence before. "What's wrong with them?" she demanded.

Fenimore stared hard at his nurse. "Pride," he said.

. . .

All the way home, Fenimore blamed the police, Mrs. Doyle, but most of all—himself, for incompetence in the Pancoast case.

"The only person who's helping me with this case," he moaned to his car's interior, "is the murderer—by systematically eliminating the suspects—one by one."

CHAPTER 30

Horatio was in the cellar practicing some new moves he planned to teach the ladies that night. He had set up a full-length mirror at one end of the cellar in which he could observe his technique. He was admiring a particularly complicated stance when he heard the muffled ring of the telephone in the office above his head.

"Shit!" He broke the stance and loped up the stairs.

"Dr. Fenimore's office." He hated playing secretary.

"Is the doctor in?" An elderly, female voice, slightly breathless.

"No, but I can get him for you."

"Is this Horatio?"

"Yes, ma'am."

"Oh, thank goodness. Maybe you can help me. This is Judith Pancoast. My sister Emily is feeling dizzy. I'm afraid it may be her pacemaker."

Horatio's heart started to pound and his palms began to

sweat. Why didn't the fuckin' doctor stay in his fuckin' office? "Where's Doyle?"

"Mrs. Doyle went on a day's excursion to the Marine Museum."

"Shit."

"What was that?"

"Do you know how to set up that transmitter gadget?"

"Oh yes."

"Well, do it. I'll get hold of the doctor."

"All right."

Horatio jiggled the receiver button until he heard a dial tone. He dialed the doctor's beeper number, hung up, and waited. He drummed his fingers on the desk, just the way he'd seen the doctor do. Two minutes passed before the phone rang.

"What's up?"

Horatio told him.

"You did exactly right. Emily should go to the hospital, but I know she won't. I'm going down there. I'll get the programmer. The pacemaker company will fax the report to the office and I'll stop by to pick it up. Can you hold the fort?"

Horatio ground his teeth. "I guess . . ."

"Good. I'll be there as soon as I can."

The boy replaced the receiver and drew a deep breath.

"She's in the library, Doctor." Judith led Fenimore into the comfortable, book-lined room. Emily was reclining on the chaise longue, legs outstretched, eyes closed.

"He's here, dear," Judith whispered.

Emily opened her eyes. "I knew you'd come." She smiled.

Fenimore drew a chair up to her side and felt her pulse. It was slow, but still within the normal range. The telephone report from the pacemaker company that Horatio had given him had revealed that the battery was fine and that Emily's artificial pacemaker was working well. "Now, tell me what's the trouble."

"Oh, nothing much. Just a little spell now and then."

Judith raised her eyebrows to the ceiling.

"What sort of spell?"

"A weak feeling."

"Where?"

"In my arms and legs."

"And your head?"

"My head felt light."

"Dizzy?"

She nodded.

"When was the last spell?"

"This morning. I was rearranging my bureau drawers and all of a sudden I had to sit down. That's when I asked Judith to call you."

"Do you feel dizzy now?"

"No, not now."

Fenimore took his stethoscope from his jacket pocket. The two ladies were quiet while he listened to Emily's chest. No sign of trouble now. Her heart was beating at about sixty-two beats per minute. But when her heart rate had dropped below the normal level, why had the pacemaker failed to take over? It was in good working order now. The battery was okay. There was only one possibility.

Fenimore took the programmer out of the case and examined the setting. His own heart began to race. Someone had reset the programmer to take over at a much lower rate than Emily's heart required. It had been reset to kick in when her heart rate slowed to thirty-five beats instead of fifty-five beats per minute. Whoever had reset it must have done so back in December, when he had left the programmer at Seacrest. Emily's natural pacemaker had continued to work until recently. When it failed, her dizzy spells began. Or—was it possible that *he* had made a mistake? Could he have set it wrong? With painstaking care, Fenimore reset the pacemaker to its proper rate and returned the programmer to its case.

"Is anything wrong, Doctor?" He had been quiet for so long, Emily was anxious.

"No. Everything's fine." He patted her hand. "Do you feel sleepy?"

"A little."

"Why don't you take a nap? And when you wake up I may have the answer to your problem."

"Oh, I hope so."

Fenimore stood up. "Could we pull the shades?"

"Certainly." Judith scurried over to the windows and pulled down the heavy, dark green shades. The sunlight was instantly replaced by a pale green glow. Fenimore felt as if he were under water.

"That's better."

Emily closed her eyes again.

Fenimore, a finger to his lips, ushered Judith out of the room.

In the parlor, over a cup of tea, Dr. Fenimore discussed Emily's condition with her sister. He decided not to mention his recent discovery about the programmer as he didn't want to upset her. And if *he* were to blame, he certainly didn't want Judith to know. Her faith in her physician might be destroyed forever. "Do you think that fall she had, when she broke her hip, was preceded by one of these 'spells'?" Fenimore asked her.

Judith thought back to that dreary day when they had buried the dolls. "I don't know, Doctor. She didn't mention it. But, then, you know Emily."

Fenimore nodded. They both knew Emily. A stoic by nature, she was apt to keep her symptoms to herself until they became severe. An admirable quality under many circumstances, but not when it came to illness.

"You haven't come across any new miniature scenes involving Emily, have you?"

Judith's hand fluttered to her throat. "You don't think—?"

"I don't know, but we must keep our eyes open."

"Oh, Doctor, I'm frightened."

Fenimore frowned. "Where are the dolls buried?"

"In the garden." Judith said. "Years ago, when Emily first had her pacemaker put in, we cut a little incision in her doll's chest and inserted a hearing aid battery. That was the only thing we could think of that resembled a pacemaker and was small enough. Then we sewed it up again."

Fenimore shook his head. "You two certainly are sticklers for authenticity."

Judith smiled.

They talked of inconsequential things until Mrs. Doyle came in—bursting with her day. The Marine Museum was wonderful! Full of octopus and squid. And afterwards— She stopped when she saw the doctor. "What are you doing here?"

When she heard what had transpired in her absence, she was aghast.

"Don't worry, Doyle. You needed a day off. You can't be expected to stay home every minute."

Nevertheless, she was chagrined and insisted on peeking in on Emily. She returned to report that the elderly woman was sleeping peacefully.

When Judith left the room to refill the teapot, Fenimore told Doyle about the programmer.

Her eyes widened.

"Can you show me where those dolls are buried?"

"Yes, Judith pointed out the spot to me the other day."

"Let's go."

"Where are you going?" Judith was in the doorway, bearing the steaming teapot.

Fenimore and Mrs. Doyle were forced to swallow another cup of tea and a full-course dinner before Fenimore announced that he and Mrs. Doyle would like to take a walk in the garden.

"But it's dark," Judith objected.

"That's the point," he said, "we'd like to look at the stars." He smiled at Doyle. "You can see them so much better down here than in the city."

"Well—" For a fleeting moment, Judith wondered if there was something going on between the doctor and his nurse. But she quickly banished that idea. Mrs. Doyle was at least a dozen years his senior. Still, she mused, stranger things had happened. . . .

Once in the garden, Mrs. Doyle led the doctor to the corner where the dolls were buried. The grave was shallow and he had no trouble extricating the shoe box with his hands. Fenimore had brought a small flashlight, the one he used for looking down people's throats. While he held the light, Mrs. Doyle sorted through the dolls until she found Emily's. She handed it to him.

Fenimore carefully examined the doll's small cotton chest. On the upper right-hand side was a tiny incision, as if cut with a pair of nail scissors—just the right size to insert a hearing aid battery. He poked his finger in the slit. The battery was gone.

CHAPTER 31

Fenimore sat at his desk, contemplating the list he had just made.

Suspects
1. Emily
2. Judith
3. Susanne
4. Mildred
5. Carrie
6. Frank

Which ones could have reset the programmer? Who would have enough knowledge? Emily and Judith had both watched him do it many times. But Emily wouldn't do it to herself—unless she wanted to avert suspicion and had counted on Fenimore to discover the problem and correct it before any damage was done. Far-fetched, Fenimore. Judith had the most opportunity and was certainly intelligent enough. What about the others? Susanne and Mildred both had been there the day of the karate demonstration, but they had not been in the room when he had reset Emily's programmer. However, he had left the instruction manual behind. Either of those women were intelligent enough to figure out how to reset it from the manual. And both had easy access to the house. They were in and out all the time. Then, there was Carrie. She dropped by often. She was quick and had a special interest in medical things. And she was in the room that day, along with Horatio, watching him reset the programmer. (Maybe Horatio did it! He allowed himself a small joke.) Had the Pancoast sisters included a bequest for Carrie in their wills? The trust officer he had consulted might have overlooked such a small legacy. The child needed money to help pay for her nursing studies. Fenimore didn't want to think about that. Hadn't Doyle told him the high school was helping her out? He must ask the sisters about Carrie. As for Frank, he doubted that the bartender had the mental capacity to dope out a programmer. And, now that he was no longer posing for Marie—poor Marie—Frank would have no reason to visit the Pancoast house. Of all the suspects, he was the least likely.

On the back of the same slip, Fenimore wrote:

Motives
1. Money
2. Love
3. Power
4. Revenge

Sal jumped onto his lap with a "Meow!" Translation? (Time for a body rub.) Fenimore obliged. Some of his best ideas had come to him while stroking his cat.

"Purr." (Thanks.)

He took out the sheet of information Mrs. Doyle had supplied him, headed:

Grapevine Gleanings

Talk with Mrs. Beesley: *Judith resented Emily when they were girls, because Emily was smarter and she thought Emily was her father's favorite. Emily resented Judith when they were young because Judith was prettier. Edgar resented both Emily and Judith when he was young, because they babied him, dressed him up in fancy clothes, and tried to curl his hair.*

Talk with Carrie: *Mildred hated Pamela because she was smarter and better educated and looked down on her. Tom and Mildred's marriage was rocky. They were always having rows over her astrology and his drinking. Adam and Mildred couldn't stand each other. Adam considered Mildred a fool. And Mildred thought Adam—a prig.*

Talk with Frank (over a cold beer!): *Marie was a saint. Edgar had been "damned" lucky to get her. Frank had been "sweet on her" in high school. He hoped her husband had appreciated her. Tom was okay. Mildred was "an ass." Susanne was a decent sort. Adam was a teetotaler. (The worst sin.)*

So much for motives. Fenimore paused in his body rub. "Meow!" (More.) He resumed his ministrations briefly. Then,

179

without apology, he rose—causing Sal to leap to the floor. "Grrr." (Not enough.) A flick of her tail. (I'll be back.)

Fenimore went to the phone and dialed the Pancoast house. After a brief talk with Emily he ascertained that both she and Judith had included a small bequest in their wills for Carrie. But, she assured him, they had never mentioned it to Carrie.

"Did Carrie know where the dolls were buried?" he asked.

Emily had no idea.

He placed a second call.

"Yes?" There was the sound of a child crying in the background.

"This is Dr. Fenimore. I wonder if you could help me? I didn't want to bother the Pancoasts and . . ."

"Yes?" she said again louder, to be heard over the noise.

"Where are the dolls?"

"What was that, Doctor? Quiet, Eddie!"

"The Pancoasts' dolls, do you know where they are?"

"I think they hid them or something. They used to be in the closet."

"But you don't know where they are now?"

"Eddie, stop that racket. No, I'm sorry Doctor. I haven't a clue."

"Thank you, Carrie." He hung up. Of course she could be lying, but her denial had the ring of truth to it and he was satisfied.

But Fenimore's satifaction was short-lived. He may have eliminated two suspects, but that still left four. He ran his hand through his hair. If only he had someone to talk to. Sal was a good companion, but she had her limitations.

From the windowsill, his cat sent him a cold stare.

With a sigh, he settled down and began a letter to Jennifer. It was easier without Mrs. Doyle peering over at him. But he found it hard to write about the Pancoast case. No matter how he phrased it, he came out in a very poor light. When he had finished, he sat for some time staring at the opposite wall. Not a good sign.

"Hey, Doc! Where should I put this?"

Fenimore, deep in thought, had not heard Horatio come in. The boy was standing in the doorway balancing something flat and round.

" 'Simple Simon met a pie-man going to the fair . . .' " he sang out.

"You know that?"

"What d'ya think, my mom didn't know Mother Goose? I got the whole fuckin' crew—Georgie Porgie, Baa Baa Black Sheep, Little Bo-Peep—"

"Okay, okay." Fenimore was laughing. What was it about this kid that always made him feel better?

Horatio laid the pie gently on his desk and removed the foil cover. As they say in the commercials, the crust was golden brown and the aroma—straight from heaven. Fenimore reached out and touched it. It was still warm.

"My mom made it for you. Apple-raisin." Horatio smacked his lips. "And here's a note." He flipped him a powder blue envelope with "Dr. Fenimore" written in a fine, cursive hand across the front.

"Take this to the kitchen"—Fenimore waved the pie away— "before I eat the whole thing right now." He tore open the note.

Dear Dr. Fenimore,

I was terribly upset that my boy, Ray, should bring you here. If I hadn't been out of my senses, I would have sent you away. If I am ever sick again I have told Ray to call the police and I will take my chances at the big hospital. I would never want you to come to such a neighborhood again. Which brings me to the reason for this letter. Where is my bill? I have saved the money and waited and waited. All I need to know is the amount. Please send the bill home with Ray.

Very truly yours,
Bridget Lopez

P.S. My boy thinks the world of you!

All this was written in the most beautiful, Catholic school script, in blue ink.

"What did she say?" Horatio, returning from the kitchen, looked anxious.

"None of your business." Fenimore grabbed a sheet of stationery and a pen from his desk drawer. In a much less legible hand, he began:

Dear Mrs. Lopez,

Thank you for the beautiful apple-raisin pie. I will probably eat it in one gulp for dinner.

As for the bill, you must leave that to me. One of the reasons I am in solo practice is because no one can tell me how to treat my patients, or how to bill them. From your son, I know that

*you are an independent sort yourself, therefore I'm sure you
will understand.*

    I am happy you have made such a complete recovery.

Sincerely,

Andrew B. Fenimore, M.D.

Fenimore glanced over at Horatio. The boy was slumped in a
chair, wearing a surly expression, doing absolutely nothing.

With a flourish, Fenimore added a postscript: *P.S. Your son
is a great asset to my office.*

He stuffed it in an envelope, wrote "Mrs. Lopez" on the
front, and sealed it. "Here. Put this in your pocket and give it
to your mother."

Horatio screwed up his face.

"What's the matter?"

"I hate secrets."

"What's secret?" Fenimore tried not to look guilty.

"Why won't you let me see it?"

"It's a private correspondence between your mother and me."

"What did she say about me?"

In exasperation, he thrust her note at him.

As the boy came to the end of the note, a dark flush spread
over his face.

"Don't worry," Fenimore laughed. "I won't hold it against
you. Come on, it's time for your lesson. Today I'm going to
teach you about CVAs, otherwise known as 'strokes.'" He sat
down next to the boy and began to explain in elementary terms
a complex article he had just finished reading in *JAMA*.

. . .

183

Horatio had no trouble finding out the contents of Fenimore's note to his mother. Mrs. Lopez showed it to all her friends and relatives, taking special pains to point out the postscript to them. She would have framed it and hung it on the wall next to "The Doctor" poster, if Horatio hadn't threatened, coldly and calmly, to kill her.

CHAPTER 32

APRIL

March merged into April. Since Adam's body had not been recovered, a memorial service was held for him at the small Presbyterian church in which generations of Pancoasts had been Christened, married, and memorialized. Gradually Susanne began to realize that her suffering was harming her children. For their sakes, she determinedly weaned herself from her tranquilizers. Mildred's nervous condition, on the other hand, steadily worsened. Mrs. Doyle noticed a tremor in her hand whenever she lifted a glass or cup, and a quiver in her voice whenever she spoke, which was seldom.

The flamboyant costumes she formerly favored had given way to an old, stained raincoat. Wrapped in this drab garment, she had taken to sitting on the boardwalk, alone, for hours at a time.

One day, Mrs. Doyle was taking a brisk walk on the board-walk (following Dr. Fenimore's prescription), when she spied

Mildred emerging from a shabby storefront which bore a sign reading:

MADAM ZORA

—PSYCHIC—

TAROT & PALM READINGS

$5.00

"Madam Zora is open early this year," said Mrs. Doyle.

"She's open all year round," Mildred said. "She lives upstairs." She sat down on a bench, facing the ocean.

"May I join you?" asked Mrs. Doyle.

Mildred turned a glassy stare on her. "No charge," she said.

Mrs. Doyle sat down. After a few moments of watching the green and white waves rush under the boardwalk, she asked, "What did Madam Zora have to say?"

No response.

"Were her predictions good?" She raised her voice to be heard over the noise of the surf.

No answer.

"It's a bit chilly." Mrs. Doyle drew her wool coat more tightly around her. Mildred was dressed even less warmly—in a thin raincoat and sandals with no stockings. "Why don't you come back to town with me and have a cup of tea?" she said.

"What?"

"A cup of hot tea?" Mrs. Doyle felt as if she were talking to a deaf person. "Would you like to have one with me?" she shouted.

"You don't have to shout." Mildred frowned. But as Mrs.

Doyle rose to leave, Mildred rose too and followed her along the weathered wooden boards to the street.

The tea shop, like Madam Zora's, stayed open all winter. It felt cozy and warm after the chill of the boardwalk. Mrs. Doyle found a table for two near a window and ordered, "A pot of tea and a plate of cakes, please."

While they waited for their order, the nurse didn't attempt to make conversation. Mildred fiddled with the menu, the silverware, and her napkin. Suddenly she looked directly at Mrs. Doyle. "I'm surprised you aren't afraid to drink tea with me."

Mrs. Doyle was taken aback.

"It has to be one of us." Mildred's tone was flat. "Emily, Judith, Susanne, or me. We're the only ones left. Who do you think it is?"

It was Mrs. Doyle's turn to be silent.

"You must have some idea!" Her voice rose.

"I wish I did, Mrs. Pancoast, but—"

"Aren't you afraid I'll slip some poison in your cup?"

The people at a neighboring table glanced their way.

Mrs. Doyle smiled. "Not at all. I'm a natural-born risk taker."

"Aries?"

She nodded.

"Well, I'm Gemini. And I'm scared shitless."

"Why don't you and the children come up to the big house and stay for a while," suggested Mrs. Doyle. "It must be very lonely—"

"You must be kidding." Her eyes blazed. "I'll never set foot in that death house again."

The waitress set down a pot of tea and a plate of cakes and hastily left them.

Mrs. Doyle poured the tea. She took a sip before she spoke. "How are your children?" she asked pleasantly.

"Well enough—considering." She paused. "They miss their dad."

Mrs. Doyle nodded sympathetically. "Of course they do."

Mildred's eyes suddenly filled. "So do I."

Mrs. Doyle reached across the table to press her hand. Mildred snatched it away and began picking her paper napkin to shreds. Finally she said, "I think Madam Zora saw something. Something . . . she was afraid to tell me. That's why she—"

"Now listen to me, Mildred"—in her anger Mrs. Doyle used the younger woman's first name—"Madam Zora is a charlatan. She knows no more about the future than you or I—"

"That's what you think!" Mildred jumped up, almost knocking over her chair, and stalked out of the restaurant.

Mrs. Doyle threw some money on the table and hurried after her, leaving a room full of gaping customers.

When she caught up with Mildred, the nurse apologized. "I'm sorry. I shouldn't have said that. Everyone has a right to their beliefs. Won't you come up to the house for dinner at least? Judith is such a good cook. And she always makes more than we can eat. We could pick up the children on the way—"

To Mrs. Doyle's surprise, Mildred acquiesced. "Never mind the children. I'll call the sitter and ask her to stay on."

The woman's moods were as erratic as the spring weather.

As they made their way up the hill, the wind died down and the little seacoast town was bathed in a warm yellow light. The light that often precedes a beautiful sunset, or—a sudden storm. Sure enough, as they walked, the sky behind the Pancoast house turned pink, lavender, and gold. The turrets and cupola and lacy gingerbread were etched vividly against the changing sky. It was a peaceful moment.

Mrs. Doyle opened the front door with the key Emily had given her. The hall was dark. The aunts had forgotten to turn on the lights. She found the switch. The vast hall seemed even larger—with the dollhouse gone. She turned to take Mildred's coat and was startled by her stillness. Her eyes were fixed on something on the platform where the dollhouse had been. Mrs. Doyle followed her gaze. Something small and white, like a scrap of paper, rested there.

Mildred moved toward it.

Mrs. Doyle followed.

Mildred bent to examine it. She clutched her throat. "No." She backed into Mrs. Doyle. "No." She clawed at the front door knob. The door fell open. "No, no, no," she moaned as she ran down the hill.

Mrs. Doyle turned to look at the object. A small, porcelain bathtub—one of the few things which could have survived the dollhouse fire. It was full of water. On the bottom lay a clothespin. Beside the tub, as if casually tossed there by its occupant, lay a tiny volume which bore the intriguing title *Astrology Comes of Age.*

I will get a doll dressed like a policeman!

—*The Tale of Two Bad Mice* by Beatrix Potter

CHAPTER 33

Mrs. Doyle did not know what to do next. Run after Mildred? Wake the aunts? They usually took naps at this time. Call the police? Call Dr. Fenimore? Her quandary was resolved by the sudden appearance of Emily at the top of the stairs.

"Oh, it's you, Mrs. Doyle. I thought I heard someone." She drew nearer and saw Mrs. Doyle's face. "Is something wrong?"

Mrs. Doyle pointed to the bathtub.

Emily descended the stairs slowly, one at a time. When she saw the tub and its contents, her hand went to her throat too. But her "No!" was softer than Mildred's.

Mindful of her heart condition, Mrs. Doyle helped her to a chair and went to look for Judith.

Unable to find her, she came back to ask Emily if she had seen her sister.

"Oh, I forgot to tell you. She took the afternoon bus to Ocean City. She needed some spices for some exotic new recipe she's trying."

She wished Judith had stayed home. She could have used her help.

Assured that Emily's heart had withstood this latest jolt of bad news, Mrs. Doyle went to telephone Dr. Fenimore. When she had told him everything, she asked what she should do.

"Call Mildred's house. Make sure she made it home safely. Call the police and ask them to come get the bathtub. Don't touch it. And don't let anyone else touch it."

"Of course not."

"And, Doyle, after the police have gone, I want you to go and stay with Mildred for the night."

"Right, Doctor."

"And for God's sake don't let her take a bath!"

"Oh, I'm sure she'll stick to showers for the rest of her life."

"It's up to you to make sure she has a long one."

"Shower?"

"No." Pause. "Life."

The police took longer than Mrs. Doyle expected. The fuss was over the tiny water-filled bathtub. If they picked up the tub to empty it, they might smudge any fingerprints adhering to the outside. The question was—how to remove this evidence with the water still inside? Mrs. Doyle came to the rescue. She disappeared into the kitchen and reappeared with a plastic syringe, the kind for basting a turkey. Deftly, she sucked the water out and, with the tip of the syringe, shoved the miniature tub into a string shopping bag. Satisfied, the officers left, swinging the bag between them.

"Wait—" Mrs. Doyle had a sudden thought and ran after

them. "Could you send an officer to guard Mildred Pancoast's house this evening?"

They nodded.

"And another one up here to guard the Misses Pancoasts?"

They looked uncertain. "It's still off-season," one officer said, "and we're understaffed."

"Well, do what you can." Mrs. Doyle waved them on.

After they left, Mrs. Doyle told Emily that Dr. Fenimore wanted her to spend the night with Mildred. "Do you mind staying here alone until Judith comes home?"

"Not at all," Emily said. "Judith will be back in an hour or so."

Mrs. Doyle threw a few things into an overnight bag and hurried out.

When Mrs. Doyle reached Mildred's house, Mrs. Perkins was waiting in the hall, with her hat on. "I didn't like to leave her alone," she whispered. "She's in such a state."

"Don't worry." Mrs. Doyle put down her overnight bag. "I'll take care of her."

The children were asleep. Mildred was huddled in a chair, wrapped in a blanket, although the night was mild. She was studying some Tarot cards, which were spread out on a card table.

Mrs. Doyle asked Mildred where she would like her to sleep.

She shrugged, never lifting her eyes from the cards.

Mrs. Doyle made her way through the one-story house, looking for a spare bed. She found one in the baby's room. The baby was sleeping peacefully. She set her bag on the end of the bed and went back to the living room. Mildred was poised exactly as she had left her.

Mrs. Doyle settled into a comfortable chair. She took out her knitting, suspecting it would be a long night. She had barely completed one row when the telephone rang. Mildred made no move to answer it. Mrs. Doyle lifted the receiver. Emily. Judith had not returned on the six-thirty bus. Mrs. Doyle looked at her watch. After seven. Although she admired the spunk and independence of elderly people today, sometimes she wished they would stay home with their knitting as her grandmother used to do.

"Have you called the bus terminal? Maybe there was a delay."

"Yes, I called. They said the buses were running on schedule."

Mrs. Doyle frowned. "I don't like you up there by yourself." She glanced at Mildred. "But I can't leave now. Could Susanne come stay with you?"

"Susanne took the children to the dentist and out to dinner in Ocean City. They won't be back until late."

Mrs. Doyle sighed. "Well, the police did say they would try to send someone along. Stay close to the phone and if anything unusual comes up, call me. I'm sure Judith will be on the next bus." As she hung up, she felt uneasy.

Mildred still brooded over her cards.

"See anything interesting?" Mrs. Doyle asked, referring to the cards.

Mildred looked at her as if she had never seen her before.

"You look tired, dear. Why don't you go to bed. I have a

sedative here for you." Mrs. Doyle patted her pocketbook. "Dr. Fenimore prescribed it."

"No, thanks." Mildred spoke shortly.

"Why not?"

"No sedatives. I have to stay awake. I have to be on guard. I have to see them coming. . . ."

"That's why I'm here," Mrs. Doyle adopted her most soothing nurse's tone. "I'll do the watching while you sleep."

"How do I know *you* won't fall asleep?"

"I'm a nurse. It's my job to stay awake. I'm used to it."

"I don't trust you. The minute I go to sleep, you'll go to sleep too."

Mrs. Doyle was not used to being distrusted. "Mrs. Pancoast, I promise you. I'm a night owl. A late-night-TV junkie." She got up and flicked on the set. "I promise, I will not blink an eye until you and the children get up in the morning."

Mildred said no more, apparently absorbed in the family sitcom on the screen. It was too stupid even for Mrs. Doyle— who loved sitcoms. She concentrated on her knitting. The next show was a little better. A thriller. During a commercial break, she noticed Mildred was dozing. As if feeling her gaze, Mildred woke with a start and disappeared toward the back of the house. Mrs. Doyle assumed she had gone to bed, until the hammering began.

Mrs. Doyle dropped her knitting and followed the sound. It was coming from the bathroom. She looked in. Kneeling beside the bathtub was Mildred. A piece of plywood lay across the top of the tub. She was trying to secure it with nails. Unfortunately, the tub was made of a slippery plastic and the nails slid or bounced but refused to penetrate.

"Please, Mrs. Pancoast. Come to bed. We can get someone to take care of that in the morning."

"No!" she shouted. "I have to do it tonight."

"Shhh. You'll wake the children." As if on cue, the baby began to cry and the two older children appeared in the doorway.

"Mommy, what are you doing?" Tommy Junior asked sleepily.

Molly stared, heavy-lidded, her thumb in her mouth.

"I'm saving my life," she yelled. "I'm trying to save your mother's life!" Once again she tried to force the nails into the plastic and watched helplessly as they skittered to the floor.

Simultaneously both children began to cry.

Mrs. Doyle went quickly to her overnight bag and took out a syringe. Thank heavens she had thought to bring it. She went back to the bathroom. As she approached, Mildred screamed, "Get away from me. Look at that needle, children. She's trying to kill me!"

The little boy threw himself against Mrs. Doyle, pummeling her with his small fists. But she managed to plunge the needle into his mother's arm.

"Oh, my God, she's killed me. Oh, my God," Mildred wailed. The children gaped in horror as their mother slumped forward on the plywood and the hammer fell with a smack on the tiles.

It took Mrs. Doyle over an hour to quiet the children and settle the baby down. The next step was to get Mildred into bed. Not a simple task. She was a tall, big-boned woman. Mrs. Doyle half dragged, half shoved her in stages, pausing frequently to catch her breath. Thank heavens the house was on one level. When she reached Mildred's bedroom, she raised her slowly, inch by inch, until her torso was resting on the counterpane. With a tremendous effort, she lifted her legs and swung her lower half up onto the bed. With a sigh, Mrs. Doyle sat down on the end of the bed and took several deep breaths. She was really too old for this kind of thing. If it hadn't been for the karate classes, she would never have been able to do it. She tucked a blanket around Mildred and slowly made her way back to the living room.

Despite her exhaustion, she was determined to stay awake all night. She had promised. And Mrs. Doyle did not take her promises lightly. Speaking of promises, where was that police officer who was supposed to come guard them? When she felt herself growing drowsy, she got to her feet and moved around the living room, tidying up. She threw away empty soda cans and picked up stray toys. She gathered astrology magazines into neat piles and dusted the New Age crystal on its pedestal above the TV. When she came to the card table, she glanced at the cards Mildred had laid out. The only one turned face up was captioned the Tower. There was a picture of a brick tower being struck by lightning. Mrs. Doyle went to the bookcase. The shelves were full of books on the occult. She pulled out a small volume entitled *Tarot* and flipped to a picture of the Tower.

"The Tower," she read, "represents unexpected upheavals and reversals. It illustrates the sudden intervention of fate in our lives, which can turn everything upside down. . . . "

She put the book away and swept the Tarot cards into a neat pack. She was about to close the spiral notebook which lay open on the table, when her eye was caught by today's date and the scribbled words:

Dear Diary,

I'm next.

She felt a sudden rush of sympathy for the tormented woman down the hall.

Letterman had barely begun his opening monologue when a neighbor's dog began to bark. Mrs. Doyle decided to check the windows and doors to make sure they were locked. They weren't. People in small towns didn't believe in locking up. Even today. One window was wide open. The bathroom window. Funny. She hadn't noticed that before. But then, during Mildred's hysterical scene, she couldn't trust her memory of anything.

At midnight, Emily called. She apologized for calling so late, but she thought Mrs. Doyle would like to know that Judith had come home. (Good heavens, during all the uproar, she had forgotten about Judith.) She had missed the last bus from Ocean City, Emily told her, and had taken a cab. She was very sorry she hadn't called.

In some ways, thought Mrs. Doyle, the elderly were like children.

A few minutes later the doorbell rang. "Who is it?" she called out.

"Seacrest Police."

She opened the door a crack. A young man in uniform stood

on the front step. "Better late than never," she said.

"I would have come sooner," he apologized with a lopsided grin. "I was tied up with some rowdy teenagers on the beach."

He looked like a teenager himself. But not rowdy. Mrs. Doyle let the young man in.

The two of them played pinochle until dawn.

Before anyone stirred, Mrs. Doyle called Dr. Fenimore. He made the necessary arrangements to have Mildred committed to a sanitarium for observation. When the attendants arrived, Mildred was too groggy to resist them. Kindly and efficiently, they bundled her into their van. After she had gone, Mrs. Doyle called Mrs. Perkins. Fortunately, she was free and could take care of the children for an indefinite period. It was after ten o'clock when the nurse finally arrived back at the aunts' house. She crawled into bed and fell into a deep sleep.

She awakened to the sound of Judith's voice telling her gently that dinner was ready. She had prepared a special dish. (The reason for the spice trip, no doubt.) How is it, she wondered, that through all the fear and turmoil and deaths, they still managed to eat? Our instinct for survival was very strong, she decided.

Eagerly, Mrs. Doyle made her way down to the dining room.

But the nurse said, "I will set a mouse-trap."

—*The Tale of Two Bad Mice* by Beatrix Potter

CHAPTER 34

I'm disappointed.

My plan was upset.

I didn't expect my intended victim to go up to the big house and see my little exhibit. That had been prepared for the benefit of the others. I had expected Mildred to come home after her walk (or rather—sit) on the boardwalk, and, as is her custom before dinner, take a long, leisurely bath. (I had observed Mildred for days and was familiar with her habits.)

Everything had been prepared. The bathroom window was unlocked. There was a thick cover of bushes below it to hide me until the appropriate time. She usually returned from her walks (sits) at about four-thirty. I had climbed in the window at four-fifteen and settled into the closet, under shelves of towels. Beneath the shelves was a deep cavity that opened into a dark cupboard under the sink. Even if someone opened the door to get a towel, it was so dark that there was small chance of being seen. It was cramped, of course. But I didn't expect to be there for more than half an hour. Forty-five minutes at the most. I had intended to wait until the victim was immersed in steamy suds with a good book. One of those astrology tomes she was so fond of. Then, I had planned to quietly emerge from the closet (located directly behind the tub), grab her around the neck, and apply enough pressure to cut off any attempt to scream. And continue the pressure until she went limp and slid under the bubbles—down, down, down—and disappeared.

Then, I would have slipped out the window and waited under cover of the bushes until dark, when I could have left unseen.

But that is not what happened. All because of nurse!

I waited and waited and waited—five o'clock, five-thirty. At five-forty the phone rang. The sitter answered it. I couldn't make out the conversation, but I suspected it was Mildred and there was a change of plans. How much longer would I have to wait? I wasn't sure my neck, back, and legs could last much longer. It was also hard to breathe. The small space under the shelves was very close. (Had I known how long I was going to be trapped there, I would have probably given myself up.) Six o'clock came and went. Six-thirty passed. At exactly six thirty-seven, Mildred came home. Barged home, I should say. She was in such a state. She burst into the bathroom. The sitter followed, trying to calm her. Peering through a crack, I saw she had a tape measure. She was taking measurements of the bathtub! She scribbled them on the back of an envelope and rushed out again. Shortly after this, I heard sawing in the backyard. The sawing went on, interrupted by obscenities, for a long time. Finally, I heard her coming back. She was dragging something heavy down the hall. When she came in the bathroom, she dropped whatever it was on top of the tub.

I peeked through the crack. A large piece of plywood covered the tub completely.

When the hammering began, I sincerely thought I would go mad. The bangs echoed—magnified a thousand times—in that small, tile-covered space. Suddenly, the banging stopped. With a flurry of curses, Mildred left the bathroom. During the next hour, I heard sounds indicating that the sitter was feeding the children and putting them to bed. At one point, the boy came into the bathroom to run water for his bath. The sitter pulled him out, murmuring, "We'll skip a bath tonight." When they were in their nightclothes, she told both children to use the toilet quickly, wash their hands, and come to bed. I wished she would do the same with their mother. Shortly afterward, the doorbell rang. I heard the sitter inform Mildred that Mrs. Doyle was here and that she planned to spend the night. It was my turn for obscenities.

There followed a long period of quiet. I had only to bear the pain of my cramped muscles and the lack of oxygen in the closet. So great was my misery, I was tempted to risk all and try to get out the window without being seen. Just then, Mrs. Doyle came in to use the facilities. After washing her hands, she opened the closet and reached for a towel. Her index finger brushed the tip of my nose. This effectively quenched any desire I had to escape. I resigned myself to unknown hours of muscular agony, not to mention possible asphyxiation.

At nine fifty-five, Mildred came back in and began hammering again. This was followed by the most ridiculous farce! Mildred and the nurse and the children all screaming at once in that small tile-covered space. (The baby was yelling in his room, too.) I thought I would have to blow my cover and come out and stop them. Suddenly there was silence. The old bag of a nurse had actually succeeded in administering a sedative to Mildred. The children started up again, of course. And the baby never stopped. But the nurse ushered the children out of the bathroom. Eventually she managed to quiet them. Even the baby. Bliss. And she dragged Mildred to her bedroom. I didn't envy her that. She was no featherweight. Now, I had nothing to worry about except my own aching bones and the lack of fresh air.

By eleven, the house was quiet. I was reasonably certain that everyone was asleep. The TV was still on. But people often fall asleep in front of the TV. I had to get out of there. At some point, during that long, tedious, tortuous evening, Mrs. Doyle had come in again to use the facilities. And on her way out, she had turned off the light. That was good. No neighbor would see me emerging from a lighted bathroom window. The stiffness and soreness of my muscles prevented me from descending with agility. I dropped clumsily into the bushes and disturbed a neighbor's dog. But his barks subsided quickly. At eleven-thirty, to the best of my knowledge, I left the premises under cover of darkness— without being seen.

As I made my way home, I had time to reflect. More than a dog had been disturbed that night. For the first time, one of my carefully laid plans had been upset. Totally disrupted, I should say. But I would make another. And I would make the disrupter pay.

Mrs. Doyle heads my list.

CHAPTER 35

Fenimore had not slept well. His dreams had alternated between Carrie and Horatio. In one, Carrie had been dragged off by Viet Cong soldiers. In another, Horatio had been mowed down by a gang of teenagers riding mammoth bicycles.

He got up, dressed, and went downstairs. Sal followed him. But she was not happy. Six A.M. was not her normal time for rising. He made a cup of tea and carried it into his office. Sal did not even bug him for her breakfast. She settled into his battered armchair and went back to sleep.

Around eight o'clock Fenimore stretched, yawned, and closed the thick, red tome, *Harrison's Textbook of Medicine*, and ambled out to the kitchen. Sal stretched, yawned, and followed him. With a paper cup he scooped some Kitty Chow out of a bag and poured it into her metal dish. The hard pellets hitting the sides sounded like machine gun fire. When he poured his own Grape—Nuts into a china bowl, they sounded much the same. He turned on the radio. Jointly munching, they listened to the news. Or rather, the lack of news. It was a quiet month globally. This month, all the action was on the home front.

And he was doing *nothing* about it!

He hurled the china bowl at the sink. It glanced off and crashed to the floor. Sal jumped. Cautiously, she went to examine the scattered bits and shards. Fenimore snatched her up and carried her out of the room before she could cut her feet.

CHAPTER 36

Jennifer made her way down the slice of beach she had discovered, far from the throngs of tourists. She had chosen this secluded spot to read her latest letter from Andrew undisturbed. When she began his letter she was quite relaxed, enjoying a peaceful moment between twilight and sunset. A well-deserved respite, after a day spent haggling with booksellers in French, a language in which she was far from fluent. But as she read on she began to grow uneasy. The Pancoast case was not going well. There had been another murder. Five in all. Bad enough. But it was the tone of the letter that alarmed her. She had never heard her friend sound so discouraged. He seemed to take the blame for the failure to discover the murderer entirely upon himself. There wasn't a speck of banter in the whole letter.

When she finished reading the letter, Jennifer folded the pages hastily and stuffed them into her beach bag. She gathered up her towel and her sunglasses and shoved her feet into her sandals. Then, like a harried sandpiper, she scurried up the beach.

A seagull squawked. If an expert in French seagullese had been on hand, he would have interpreted the sound to mean *"Ensuite?"* (What next?).

CHAPTER 37

When Fenimore walked into Rafferty's office, the detective glanced up. "You look like the wrath of God. What's wrong? A misdiagnosis?"

"No." He grabbed a chair. "No diagnosis."

"That's worse. Tell the poor bastard to get a second opinion."

"Can't."

"Why not? I thought you docs did that all the time. Shared the responsibility. Team work. Isn't that what group practice is all about?"

"I practice solo, remember. And I don't know the patient."

Rafferty put aside the report he had been working on and looked at his friend.

"Remember the two aunts and the dollhouse murders?"

He nodded. "The one in which you were coddling some of the prime suspects?"

Fenimore winced.

"Did you get to the bottom of that?"

Fenimore shook his head. "The state police are on it now. They're into fingerprints and DNA. I can't help feeling the answer doesn't lie in the lab, but in here." He tapped his forehead.

"Meaning?"

"Meaning—the psychology of the murderer." Fenimore looked his friend in the eye. "Is there such a thing as a motiveless murder?"

Rafferty considered. "Occasionally—you run into a psychopath. Someone who murders for the fun of it. The thrill of it. Or . . . the art of it. Murder for murder's sake, you might say. But even that is a motive of sorts."

Fenimore nodded. "De Quincy wrote a whole essay on the art of murder."

Rafferty rolled his pen between his palms. "No, Fenimore, when you get down to it, there is no such thing as a motiveless murder. Even a psychopath has his reasons—warped though they may be. No one murders for nothing."

Fenimore sighed.

"Your murderer has a motive, all right. You just haven't uncovered it."

"I suppose you're right." Fenimore sounded exhausted. "But can't a motive be unconscious? I mean, there must be murderers who are in the dark about their own motives. Take Gregory Peck in *Spellbound*, for instance. It took horrendous efforts on Bergman's part to uncover his motive."

"But he wasn't the murderer, remember? He just thought he

211

was. That old chestnut was the theme of that film—you can't commit a crime while drugged or under the influence that you wouldn't commit when you're sober."

"You disagree?" asked Fenimore.

"Emphatically. In real life your hard drinker commits plenty of crimes he wouldn't dream of when he's sober. So does the druggie. It's bullshit." He jabbed his memo pad with his pen. "Now, you're getting into the realm of criminal psychology. Would you like to talk to one of our experts?"

"Can't hurt."

Rafferty pressed a buzzer on his desk and spoke into his intercom. "Is Dr. Landers in?"

"I think so," came the rasping reply.

"Ask the doctor to step into my office."

"Yes, sir."

While waiting for Dr. Landers, they discussed the ball scores. The Phillies were enjoying an early spring spurt. Rafferty was elated. Fenimore predicted doom later in the season.

"You asked to see me?" A tall, blond woman in a trim navy suit stood in the doorway.

"Dr. Landers, come in. This is my friend, Dr. Fenimore."

"The famous investigator?"

Fenimore coughed. "Unofficially."

"You've solved a number of very difficult crimes—unofficially." She smiled, shaking his hand warmly.

"Right now he's involved in a case he can't solve," Rafferty said maliciously. (He was a trifle put out by Dr. Landers's open admiration for his friend.) "He has a question for you. Is there such a thing as a murderer with no motive? Or, at least, no conscious motive?"

She frowned. "Oh yes. The motive can be totally uncon-scious. For example, if they suffer from multiple personalities, it's possible for them to commit a crime in the guise of one personality and have no memory of it or motive for it when under the guise of another personality." She sat down in the chair Fenimore hurriedly drew out for her. Rafferty noticed (and not for the first time) that even the most liberated females never objected to Fenimore's old-fashioned courtesies. Even though he wasn't much to look at, he had a certain charm with women.

"I ran into such a case just recently," the psychiatrist contin-ued. "A respectable businessman murdered his wife. He had a second personality—that of a hardened criminal. One day he mistook his wife for an informer and shot her. When he woke up, or rather, returned to his businessman personality, he was horrified to find his wife dead. He had no memory of having killed her. And, of course, the businessman had no motive for killing her."

"Fascinating," murmured Fenimore. "Does premeditation play any part in such murders?"

"Oh no," Dr. Landers said. "Their murders are almost always unplanned and impulsive. And—there's usually no attempt at concealment afterward. The murderer is in a state of shock or trauma over what he or she has done."

"I see." Unfortunately, this description did not fit a murderer who preceded each murder with a meticulously arranged scene in a dollhouse.

"I have a book in my office describing such cases. I'd be glad to lend it to you," Dr. Landers offered.

"I'd appreciate that."

"Perhaps we could discuss this over lunch," she added, preceding him through the door.

He was half out the door when Rafferty stopped him.

"Some free medical advice, Doc. No late lunches. What you need is a long nap." He winked. "Alone," he added.

Rafferty, a happily married man, was under the misapprehension that Fenimore, a bachelor, led a full and varied sex life. Nothing could have been farther from the truth. But he was not about to enlighten his friend. "Thanks," he said. "Send me a bill."

Rafferty waved him away.

Fenimore took the first part of Rafferty's advice. No lunch. Not in deference to Rafferty, but because he wanted to get on with his case and he thought the type of criminal Dr. Landers had described was a dead end. He was convinced now that the Pancoast murderer had only one personality—a single, diabolical one—and a definite motive. It was up to him to find it. Only then would he be able to identify the murderer.

Out of courtesy, he read a few of the case histories in Dr. Landers's book. But he soon laid it aside and began to doodle on his scratch pad. He scribbled the names:

Emily
Judith
Mildred
Susanne

After leaving a space, he added halfheartedly:

Frank
Carrie

Beside each name, he wrote "motive" and drew a large question mark in the style of each person. Emily's was slender and willowy, Judith's—rounded and sturdy, Susanne's—tailored and conventional, Frank's—robust and strong, Mildred's—flashy and flamboyant, Carrie's—perky and sharp.

Then, following the second part of Rafferty's advice, he fell sound asleep in his chair.

He woke abruptly, heart pounding. He had dreamed he was surrounded by giant question marks resembling sickles—blood dripping from their blades. Slowly, they were closing in on him.

He did not need Dr. Landers to interpret his dream.

CHAPTER 38

MAY

Jennifer pulled at her skirt, ran her hand through her newly cropped hair, and pressed the bell. She hadn't seen him for several months and he wasn't expecting her. She was about to press the bell again when the door opened.

"Hey!" Horatio.

"Hey," she replied weakly.

"Come on in." He stepped back to let her pass. "Nobody's home." He followed her into the waiting room. "Doyle's at the Shore and Doc's making rounds. How's Europe?"

"Still intact."

"Meet any Frenchmen?"

Jennifer thought of the string of ancient, garrulous booksellers she had wined and dined in an effort to acquire rare books. "A few."

"Cool."

Sal looked up from her place on the windowsill.

"Hi, Sal." Jennifer waved.

The cat looked away, out the window.

"She's a moody old thing," Horatio apologized, rubbing Sal's head. He sprawled on the sofa. "You're back early, aren't ya?"

Jennifer sat rather stiffly on her straight-backed chair. "A little."

"Can I getcha something?" He suddenly recognized his position as host.

"I *am* thirsty. Would he have a Coke?"

"I'll check." He disappeared to the kitchen. Jennifer heard him breaking ice from a tray. She went to join him.

"You don't have to wait on me." She grabbed a glass from the cupboard and held it out to receive the ice cubes. As he was returning the tray, she caught sight of the contents of the freezer compartment. A steak and a box of French fries. Below, in the refrigerator part, nestled among the cans of Coke, lay a jug of cheap wine. (Fenimore had simple tastes.)

They took their drinks back to the waiting room. Horatio drank his from the can. "Did you eat a lot of crap suzettes and stuff?" He stretched out on the sofa.

"I had horse meat in Paris."

Horatio made an unattractive gagging noise.

"It's really very good. You wouldn't be able to tell it from cow meat if it weren't for the signs."

"Signs?"

"In France, if a restaurant serves horse meat they have to display a sign out front with a horse's head. It's usually painted gold or bronze."

Horatio shook his head. "How could you eat it?" His acquaintance with horses was limited to those ridden by members of the Philadelphia police force (which he observed from a respectful distance) and the sorry nags that pulled the buggies full of tourists around Independence Hall.

"Cows are nice too," she said.

"I've never seen a cow."

Suddenly, Jennifer was acutely aware of the confines of Horatio's world. He had probably never been to a farm. He had probably never seen the ocean either.

"I've seen an elephant though. My dad took us to the zoo once."

"I've never tried elephant," Jennifer said blandly. "But in this town in Italy, I had ravioli at a little restaurant. It was delicious. But when I came out I passed the door to the kitchen. It was wide open, and hanging on the wall from hooks, skinned and waiting for the meat grinder, were three cats!"

Sal stopped in the midst of a wash and stared at Jennifer.

Horatio laughed. "She heard that."

Jennifer heard something else. A key in the lock. She sat more rigidly upright.

"There's the doc," Horatio said, unnecessarily.

When Fenimore came down the hall, the three occupants of the waiting room looked at the doorway expectantly. As always, the doctor paused to glance in and see if there was a stray patient he should greet. He didn't see Jennifer at first. Her chair was off to his right.

"Look who blew in." Horatio nodded at Jennifer.

He turned.

"I came back a little early," she murmured apologetically. "Dad was tired of baked beans and tuna and sent me an SOS."

"Well . . ." Fenimore pulled himself together and spoke heartily. "That's great. Why don't we all go out and celebrate." He included Horatio and Sal with the sweep of his hand.

But Jennifer had caught his first look and her self-confidence was restored. She sent Horatio a warning glance.

"Sorry, man." The boy rose languidly. "I have plans." He disappeared down the hall toward the front door. They didn't speak until the door slammed behind him.

"What do you feel like? French, Italian?" he asked.

"You know," she said, "I've had my fill of Continental cuisine. What I really crave is something American."

"Cheese steak?" He grinned.

"Well, maybe not quite that. How about a juicy steak, French fries, and a bottle of wine?"

Fenimore was thoughtful. "In that case, I don't think we need to go out. I have all those ingredients right here."

"What a coincidence." Jennifer maintained a poker face.

"But the steak is frozen," he said.

"How long will it take to defrost?"

"An hour or so."

"We could start on the wine."

"Don't move." Fenimore disappeared into the kitchen. When he returned with two glasses brimming with wine, Jennifer had moved onto the sofa. She looked especially well, he thought. She had a slight tan, picked up on the Mediterranean beaches. Her eyes seemed to have picked up some of the intense blue of the Mediterranean Sea as well. And her hair was different. Close-cropped, revealing the lovely curve of her head. Setting the glasses down on a table covered with last year's

219

magazines, he joined her on the sofa. On impulse, he ran his hand down the back of her head. "New cut?"

She nodded.

"Paris?"

She nodded again.

"Too bad."

Her eyes widened.

"It can't be repeated."

"I can always go back."

"Not right away."

"No . . ."

Sal, deciding enough was enough, jumped from the windowsill and padded over to the sofa, careful to give Jennifer a wide birth. (She had not forgotten the ravioli story.) She leapt onto the vacant cushion next to Fenimore and rubbed her head against his thigh.

"Hey!" Fenimore reached back with one hand to remove her.

"Careful!" Jennifer warned. "She's jealous."

Fenimore let go of Jennifer and placing both hands under Sal's forelegs, raised her to eye level. "You're not jealous, are you?"

"Growrrr!" She snarled and twisted.

He dropped her like a hot potato.

"I told you." Jennifer was lounging back on the sofa, observing them through narrowed lids. She looked like a cat herself— a fragile, blue-eyed feline.

"How much do you weigh?" He surveyed her.

"What a question."

"Seriously."

"About a hundred and twelve."

In his mind's eye, Fenimore compared her to an equivalent weight at the gym. Jennifer's weight was distributed differently, of course. Without warning, he scooped her up and started for the stairs.

"What are you doing?"

"Testing my strength."

"But it's not good for you."

He halted mid-stairs, his expression grim. "I'm too old?"

"Heavens, no," she said quickly. "But you're not in shape."

A glint came into his eye.

"Andrew?" She stared up at him from the crook of his arm. "You haven't been working out?"

Suddenly shy, he nodded.

"What's come over you?"

"What would you do, if you were suddenly surrounded by two fitness freaks and a bunch of Olympic octogenarians?"

"The karate class?"

He nodded.

"Poor Andy." She reached up and patted his cheek.

"Enough." He strode up the rest of the stairs, carried her down the hall to his bedroom, and dumped her unceremoniously on the bed.

"What have you been doing while I was away? Reading *Gone With the Wind*?"

He grinned evilly and sat down on the bed. "I may not look like Clark Gable, but . . ." He caught her up in a smothering embrace.

Jennifer laughed.

He drew back abruptly. "What's the matter?"

"Nothing. It's just . . . you're so different."

He held out his arm and flexed his biceps.

"Good grief." She touched the sinewy bulge gingerly.

"You like it?"

"Well—"

"You don't. You prefer the wimpy type." He looked crest-fallen.

She laughed again. "You were never wimpy. It's just that I have to get used to—"

"The new me?"

She nodded.

"Let's begin." He drew her close. He could feel her heart beating against his chest. And the beats were not the normal seventy-two beats of a human. Nor even the hundred and thirty beats of a small mammal. They were the one hundred and sixty-six beats . . . of a bird.

CHAPTER 39

They had moved to Fenimore's living and dining area. Situated between the office and the kitchen, it was a pleasant, unpretentious space, furnished with an old couch, a worn oriental rug, a couple of nondescript lamps, and shelves of books. They had lit a fire in the fireplace. Although it was May, spring was late and there was a chill in the air. They had finished the steak. Their dirty dishes and empty wineglasses rested in the sink. The remains of the fire glowed in the grate. Sal, her jealous rage forgotten, dozed on the hearth. Their coffee cups were nearly empty when Jennifer asked, "What's new with the Pancoast case?"

If she had turned into a witch, doused the fire, and poured gall into his cup, she could not have destroyed Fenimore's mood more completely. For a few blissful hours he had forgotten Seacrest, the Pancoast family, the murderer who lurked in their midst, and the sorry part he was playing in the whole affair. Jennifer's unexpected return had erased all that completely from his mind. Now it came roaring back, like an angry tidal wave, full of sound and fury.

"I don't want to discuss it."

"Andrew!"

"It's hopeless. The police are bungling idiots. Even Doyle has failed me. And here I am stuck in Philadelphia, forced to wait for the next phone call to tell me about the next murder." He was pacing now.

"Can't you get someone to cover for you?"

"No." He stopped and stared down at her. "I'm a doctor first. Detecting is a hobby. I have no right to dabble in it. I'm no expert. They'd be better off without me."

"Then all they'd have is the 'bungling' police. At least with Doyle on the scene and you within call, there's a chance—"

He sat down again, his head in his hands.

"How many are left?" she asked.

He glanced up. "Emily, Judith, Mildred, Susanne." He ticked them off on one hand.

"And the children?"

"Oh my God . . ."

Jennifer was silent. After a moment she said, "What about Rafferty?"

"What about him?"

"Can't he help?"

"He's in the wrong state. All he can do is give advice."

"Have you talked to him?"

"Yes." His voice was weary.

"What did he say?"

"The usual. Mind your own business. Oh yes, and he thinks

I'm too close to the Pancoast sisters to see them objectively."

"Are you?"

He frowned. "I don't know."

They were silent.

Suddenly he said, "Do you know what 'karate' means in Japanese?"

"No."

" 'Empty hand.' In self-defense, it means—'without a weapon.' With me, it sums up my role in this case. I dove in—and came up empty-handed." He held out both hands, palms up.

She grabbed his hands.

After a moment Jennifer murmured, "I must go. Dad will think I've been mugged."

Fenimore let her go.

Jennifer went upstairs and exchanged the tent-size T-shirt Fenimore had lent her for her own blouse and skirt, and slipped her bare feet into her sandals.

When she came downstairs, Fenimore was waiting in the hall. "I'll walk you home," he said.

Although the intense glow of the early evening had faded with the fire, a small ember remained. The yellow disk of the city hall clock, the tiny white lights that decorated the trees along Broad Street, and the flickering gaslights in front of the Academy of Music all contributed to rekindling that ember. When he left her at her apartment door, his good-night embrace was unusually fervent and he mumbled into her collarbone, "Glad you're back."

CHAPTER 40

It was Memorial Day weekend. Seacrest was officially open for the summer season. The main street was decked with flags and clogged with creeping cars.

Fenimore was in one of them.

The sidewalks were packed with people in various stages of undress, tank tops and jeans, halters and shorts, swimsuits and T-shirts—or just swimsuits.

How he wished he were one of them—here on a holiday—with nothing more important to worry about than whether to have a hotdog or a cheeseburger—whether to swim or to sunbathe. Instead, he was here to investigate the murders of five people and the cause of insanity in another. Of course, he had no one to blame but himself. He didn't have to play detective. For that matter he didn't have to work as hard as he did as a physician—not in these days of HMOs and group practice. If he played the game, he could have every other weekend off. Take trips. Play golf. No one was stopping him. It was his choice. If only he didn't value his freedom so damned much. Unfortunately, like that "hardy race of barbarians" he had been reading about in Gibbon's *Decline and Fall* (Fenimore's idea of light, summer reading), he too "despised life when it was separated from freedom." So why don't you shut up, Fenimore? He pressed the accelerator and actually moved three inches without hitting the car in front of him.

Unfortunately, he knew of no shortcut to the Pancoast house. To while away the time, he studied the stream of humanity on either side of the car. The quantity of exposed skin was predominantly pale. By the end of the weekend most of it would be varying shades of pink, scarlet, and vermilion. The odor of suntan lotion, popcorn, and hot asphalt filtered to him through his inefficient air conditioning system. (He never had it repaired until it conked out entirely.) Like a magic carpet, the smell of the sea carried him back to childhood summers he had spent at the seashore. Long, limitless lazy days that all ran into each other. Whoops! Almost ran into that young woman. She had been about to edge her way between his car and the one in front, dragging two small blond boys behind her.

He rolled down the window. "Carrie!"

Her frown was instantly replaced by an incredible smile. "Doctor?" She came up to the window. "What are you doing here?"

"Decided to drive down to see the Pancoasts. Forgot it was the Big Weekend." He shrugged at the crowd.

She opened the back door, and pushing her small brothers ahead of her, got in. "I'll give you a hand," she said. "See that little side street?" She pointed a few yards in front of the car.

He nodded.

"When you get there, turn right."

Ten minutes later, he obeyed.

"Okay. Now make a left at the next corner. . . . Now a right . . . That's it. Now another left. Now look straight ahead."

There was the hill, and at the top, the rambling back of the Pancoast house.

"Well, I'll be damned."

"We'll get out now," she said, shepherding her brothers out the door.

"I'm sure glad I ran into you," Fenimore said, with feeling.

"You almost ran *over* me," she said, with a laugh.

In his rearview mirror, he watched them continue to wave as he made his way up the hill.

He hadn't told Carrie his real reasons for coming to Seacrest. The primary one was the investigation, of course. But there was a secondary one: to relieve Doyle of her nurse/companion duties and take her back to Philadelphia. Emily's hip had mended and her "spells" had disappeared as soon as he had reset her pacemaker. Doyle seemed unable to shed any further light on the Pancoast murders. Now he needed her back at the office desperately, before the Medicare authorities arrived with a warrant for his arrest.

It was a relief to leave the overcrowded village behind. To catch a glimpse of the sea—unimpeded, and a whiff of the sea—unpolluted. He pulled up to the back door.

Mrs. Doyle came out to meet him. "I was expecting you to come from the other direction," she said.

He explained about Carrie's shortcut. "If it weren't for running into that child," he said, "I'd still be down there frying like a sardine."

The aunts were waiting inside. They greeted him warmly, welcoming him as their longtime physician and friend. He wished he could return their greetings with the same enthusiasm. But now, in his mind, an ugly question mark hung over both of them.

During lunch, he was caught up on all the latest news.

The good news: Susanne had made a remarkable recovery. Once she had determined to stop the sedatives, Susanne had devoted herself to caring for her children and was also helping to care for Mildred's. She had started a small day care center in a wing of the aunts' house. The aunts were more than happy to have the wasted space put to good use. A few children from the neighborhood were attending too. But not nearly as many as Susanne would have liked. Unfortunately, the Pancoast house had acquired a taint. Some parents were afraid to send their children to the "Death House" as it was sometimes now called—in hushed tones.

The bad news: Mildred was not progressing. She spent most of her time babbling about baths—and refusing to take one. It required a nurse and two attendants to get her into the shower. They only attempted it once a week. They simply couldn't afford the extra staff required to do it more often.

Emily was crocheting an afghan.

Judith was experimenting with some new recipes. Someone had given her a wok and a wok cookbook for her birthday. On April 5 she had quietly celebrated her eightieth year.

"She's tried out every Asian dish on us," Mrs. Doyle said.

"It's a wonder we aren't all speaking Chinese," Emily said.

Judith laughed. "It keeps me busy. And my mind off . . ."

There was a painful pause. Fenimore filled it by describing an episode featuring the Red Umbrella Brigade. It seems Mrs. Dunwoody discovered that the umbrellas she had ordered for graduation were black instead of red!

"Oh no," gasped Mrs. Doyle, the only one present who fully appreciated the gravity of the situation. "What did she do?"

Fenimore smiled. "The only thing a gracious, elderly lady proficient in the martial arts could do." He paused, letting them hang. "She called the mail order house and told them to get their butts moving or she would beat them black and blue."

Mrs. Doyle breathed more easily. "But," she said, "Mrs. Dunwoody shouldn't have said 'black and blue.' One of the miracles of karate is—it leaves no mark."

"Details, details, Doyle," replied Fenimore. "Whatever she said, the red umbrellas arrived early the next morning by Federal Express."

After lunch Fenimore excused himself and hurried down to the police station to catch up on the most recent developments.

The ladies passed the afternoon more pleasantly, playing gin rummy, sipping iced tea, and dozing on the big screened porch. (Judith and Emily had both skipped their naps in order not to miss a moment with Mrs. Doyle.) But their determinedly cheerful conversation was occasionally marred by references to the nurse's imminent departure.

"How will we ever manage without you?" Emily said.

"We'll miss you so much," Judith added.

Mrs. Doyle tried to soften her leave-taking with fervent promises of return visits.

About four o'clock, Judith excused herself to prepare yet another Asian feast.

Fenimore arrived back at the house deeply discouraged. He had learned that all the experts' tests for fingerprints and DNA had been dismal failures. The murderer had eluded the most modern laboratory techniques. The solution to this case, as he had predicted, would not be found in the laboratory, but elsewhere.

Fenimore had no trouble praising Judith's dinner. It was superb. He had second helpings of everything—including two cups of sake (provided by the teetotaling aunts as a sign of their high regard for him).

After dinner, while the ladies were washing up (Fenimore had offered to help, but they had shooed him out of the kitchen), he decided to take a walk. Maybe if he gave the Pancoast case a rest, a new idea would come to him. Sometimes when you are too uptight, he rationalized, the obvious solution escapes you. Maybe if he relaxed awhile he would be more successful. He ducked under the mammoth American flag, which hung like a curtain from the porch roof, and ambled down the hill toward the town.

It was dusk. The village of Seacrest, which on a winter's night boasted only a few street lamps, was ablaze—as if charged by some super electric battery. The streets and boardwalk surged with light from shop windows, restaurants, and movie marquees. At the far end of town, where a visiting carnival had parked itself, the colorful lights of a Ferris wheel spun against the night sky. Fenimore paused to listen to the faint tinkle of the carousel. The sake had produced a light of its own inside him. Deciding to postpone any further investigations until the next morning, he headed for the inn.

The Tale of ---------------------------- ---------------------------- *

CHAPTER 41

Serving drinks, Frank greeted Fenimore like a long-lost brother. In a few minutes, the doctor was seated comfortably at the bar, surrounded by congenial villagers. Ever since that first day, when Fenimore had been forthright with them about Pamela's death, they had accepted him. Tourists didn't frequent the inn. It was too far from the boardwalk. At one time, it was a coach stop on the old turnpike and the center of all social activity. Now the inn was off the beaten track and depended mainly on local trade.

Fenimore ordered Scotch, fearing an order of sake would seem too effete for the locals. He had another. And another. For the first time in months, he felt strangely carefree. Another doctor was covering for him this weekend. He didn't have to drive home tonight. Mrs. Doyle was coming back with him on Sunday to take care of the mess at the office. And Jennifer was home. He had to admit he had missed her and was inordinately happy over her return. Of course, he still hadn't solved the

Pancoast case. But there hadn't been a murder for several weeks. Maybe the murderer was going through a midlife crisis and had decided on a career change. He allowed himself a laugh at his own black humor, drank deeply from his drink, and forgot what time it was. At some point, he lifted his glass and offered a toast to the assembled company à la Ben Jonson: "In short measures, life may perfect be. . . ."

"Here! Here!" His companions agreed.

Sometime later, as he walked up the hill (wove would be a better description) in the dark, he whistled a favorite Bohemian air which his mother had taught him. It was a merry melody she used to sing to him while supervising his bath. In translation it went:

> Don't forget your nose,
> my dear,
> And don't forget your neck.
> Be sure to wash your toes,
> my dear . . .

What was that rosy glow in the sky? Could dawn be breaking already?

> And don't forget your ears,
> my dear,
> A son with dirty ears,
> is what every mother fears,
> —a sign of Great Neglect.

He focused on his watch. The hands and digits glowed a fuzzy green. Everything was glowing. Twelve o'clock. He'd better get home before he turned into a pumpkin. What was dawn doing out at midnight? "Midnight Dawn." Was that a title to a poem? If not, he would write one. . . .

Halfway up the hill, he halted. The rosy glow was flickering. Dawn doesn't flicker.

He took a deep breath to replenish his oxygen. Mixed with the smell of the sea was the acrid smell of something burning.

CHAPTER 42

Ever since his days as an intern, Fenimore had been able to throw off the effects of sleep or alcohol at a moment's notice. He could receive an urgent call in the middle of the night from a sick patient, and answer the phone without a trace of grogginess. The few times he had become thoroughly soused and his help was needed, he had sobered up instantly. By the time Fenimore reached the brow of the hill, all outward and inward signs of inebriation had left him.

The flames were concentrated on the right side of the house. They were coming from a second-floor bedroom. Fire sirens could be heard in the distance. Someone else must have seen the glow. He was running for the front door when he collided with Judith. Barefoot, in a long nightgown, she was holding a sweater wrapped around her head. He grabbed her arm. "Where are Doyle and Emily?"

She turned toward the house and pointed to the widow's walk, which hung suspended from the burning bedroom.

Through the smoke, he could just make out two figures—a portly one, supporting a longer, slender one in her arms.

Suddenly the place was alive with yellow-slickered firemen, hauling hoses, ladders, and shouting at each other. Fenimore grabbed the arm of one and pointed to the widow's walk. Another fireman, having already taken in the scene, was fixing a ladder in place. He scuttled up the rungs while two other firemen arranged a net under the balcony. Fenimore watched the fireman lift Emily from Doyle's arms and arrange her over his shoulders in the traditional "fireman's grip." Slowly, steadily he made his way down the ladder with his burden. Cautiously, Mrs. Doyle followed close behind. As Fenimore watched, the small balcony let go of the house and fell with an explosion of sparks—to the garden below.

A noise at Fenimore's elbow made him turn. A short, bald fireman in a yellow slicker stood beside him. The fireman looked up, his face illuminated by the flames.

Judith.

A scene from the evening after Pamela's funeral flashed through Fenimore's mind. A lighted bathroom window. A drawn shade. The silhouette of a bald head moving across it. Then darkness.

The sweater which Judith had wrapped around her head to conceal its nakedness had fallen to her shoulders. A fireman must have given her his slicker to wear.

She smiled a mad smile. "I almost got them!" she cried.

Firmly, Fenimore took her elbow and steered her between the firemen and over the hoses which crisscrossed the front lawn. She made no attempt to escape. When they reached the nearest police car, he settled her into the front seat and shut the door. Walking around to the other side, he spoke in a low voice to the officer behind the wheel. "Take her down to the station and lock her up," he said. "And be careful. She's dangerous."

The officer glanced at Judith sitting calmly beside him, her hands folded in her lap. As he started the motor, he gave Fenimore an odd look.

The Tale of ----------------------------- ----------------------------- *

CHAPTER 43

JUNE

Mrs. Doyle had the Pancoast house to herself.

Neither Emily nor Mrs. Doyle had suffered any burns. Only mild respiratory irritation from smoke inhalation. Mrs. Doyle had been released from the hospital the next morning. But, because of Emily's age and cardiac history, Dr. Fenimore had insisted that she remain under observation for a few days.

Judith, of course, was in jail. Not in a cell, however. She was in the prison infirmary, in a state of shock, and she remained unresponsive to questioning.

Despite the extent of the fire, the damage had been minimal. It had broken out in the closet of Emily's room and spread to the adjoining bedroom where Mrs. Doyle had been sleeping. The firemen had managed to contain the fire in those two rooms. Judith's room, located across the hall, had been untouched.

When the smoke detector had started to bleat, Emily had cried out, alerting Judith and Mrs. Doyle. Then she had headed for the widow's walk—the nearest means of escape. Mrs. Doyle had followed her out on the balcony. When Emily succumbed to the smoke, Mrs. Doyle had caught her before she fell. Judith had made her escape down the main staircase and out the front door.

When members of Edgar's former construction firm heard of the catastrophe, they readily volunteered their services. They promised to send carpenters and electricians to repair the damage immediately. Mrs. Doyle offered to stay on to let them in, provide coffee and soft drinks, and generally supervise the repairs.

She moved into another guest room, of which there were many. Except for the loss of her clothes and an unpleasant acrid odor, she was hardly inconvenienced at all. She borrowed a housedress of Judith's, ignored the odor which the smoke and water had left behind, and under the guise of putting the house in order, searched for new evidence. Dr. Fenimore may have been satisfied with his solution of the case, but Mrs. Doyle was decidedly not. Judith Pancoast—a murderer? Ridiculous. Mrs. Doyle prided herself on her intuitive sense about people. And just as she had sensed immediately that Carrie would make a good nurse, she knew that Judith was that rare thing—an innately good person—barely capable of the smallest unkindness—let alone murder!

She had lived closely with Judith for several months, watched her considerate care of her older sister, and her sincere concern for all the other members of her family. She would have made a wonderful wife and mother. When denied this role by her father, she could have become bitter and withdrawn. Instead, she had turned her affectionate nature outward on her brother and sister, her nieces and nephews, and their children.

Mrs. Doyle was quite aware, however, that her *feeling* that Judith was innocent was not good enough. She must produce evidence to convince Dr. Fenimore and the police of their error. And enough evidence to refute Judith's damning confession: "I almost got them." No easy task. This was the primary reason Mrs. Doyle had offered to stay on at the house. If there was any evidence to be found, surely it would be found there. She had been there twenty-four hours since the fire, frantically searching, and so far had come up with nothing.

Dr. Fenimore, on the other hand, seemed satisfied with the outcome of the Pancoast case. He was distressed, of course, that the murderer had turned out to be his old patient and friend. But hadn't Rafferty, the expert, warned him of this very outcome? And if he hadn't been so hardheaded and taken the policeman's advice earlier, he might have solved the case sooner and prevented a number of deaths. He did wonder what Judith's motive might have been. The psychologist, Dr. Landers, had told him emphatically that no murder was ever committed without a motive. But he brushed this aside. When someone says loud and clear, "I almost got them," it's no time for nit-picking.

One thing did bother him. Judith's baldness. How had that escaped him? She had been his patient for years and he *had* examined her ears. How could he have missed her wig? He was chagrined. It was a matter of professional pride.

It seemed Judith had lost her hair as a child, after a severe case of scarlet fever. It was before they had become patients of Dr. Fenimore's father. And probably by design, there was no mention of it in her patient file. Emily was the only other person who knew about it. It was a dark secret. Judith had changed her wigs gradually as she grew older, wearing ones with a little gray at first, then adding more gray, and finally adopting the silver wig which she now wore. Fenimore had learned all this from Emily on one of his hospital visits.

Fenimore, in turn, had told Emily that Judith had survived the fire unharmed. But nothing more. Emily must regain her full strength before she learned the terrible truth about her sister. He was glad Emily had not inquired why Judith had not come to visit her.

Mrs. Doyle had gone to the store for just three items—milk, bread, and orange juice. But she had come home exhausted. The supermarket had been teeming with boisterous tourists and she had been forced to wait in the "Express" line for over twenty minutes while the checker validated one of their credit cards. That tourist had been buying *a single* item—a bottle of catsup. Mrs. Doyle hoped he choked on it.

Her feet hurt. Her head hurt. After putting her purchases away in the kitchen, she dragged herself up the stairs. Since the workmen had left and she had the house to herself, she decided to take a short nap before dinner.

When she came into the bedroom, she glanced in the mirror—something she rarely did. Her reflection confirmed the way she felt. Bags under her eyes, fatigue lines around her mouth. And her hair, which had a mind of its own under ordinary circumstances, had turned into a halo of corkscrews—courtesy of the damp sea air. Hunting for her comb, her eyes fell to the bureau. Next to her comb lay an assortment of small objects, forming a curious still life. The bottom half of a clothespin lay severed from its button-top. The top had been chopped off and decorated with a neat red cross. Nearby stood a bottle of nail polish of the same red hue. And beside the bottle lay a small tool. She bent to examine it. A pint-sized hatchet.

Mrs. Doyle caressed her neck gingerly.

Two days had passed since the fire. Fenimore was working late, puttering around his office, trying to make some sense out of the mountain of paperwork. Ms. Sparks had been more absorbed in "Mr. Lopez" than in her work, Fenimore thought ruefully. Yesterday's mail still lay unopened on his desk. Another stack had arrived that day. He was about to tackle the first pile when the telephone rang. Fenimore picked it up.

"Doctor . . . ?" A low, male voice—semifamiliar.

"Yes."

"This is Ben—from Ben's Variety in Seacrest."

"Oh yes, Ben. What can I do for you?"

"You'll probably think I'm crazy for calling—" He paused. "But this fellow came in a little while ago and bought a bottle of nail polish. Now, there's nothing in that. It was probably for his wife. But I didn't recognize him, and I know everybody in Seacrest—except for the tourists. And he wasn't a tourist."

"Go on."

"He didn't say anything. Just brought the bottle over to the counter and paid for it. He was wearing dark glasses and some kind of official-looking cap."

"How tall was he?"

"Average height. About five foot seven or eight inches. And thin. Very thin."

"What made you uneasy?"

"The way he was dressed, for one. As if he were in disguise or something. And the calm, deliberate way he did everything. When he walked in the store, he went straight to the cosmetic section. That's how I knew he wasn't a tourist. The tourists stumble around blindly in here, looking for things. I don't cater to the tourist trade."

"What else?"

"Well, he comes up to the counter. Opens his wallet. Counts out the exact amount very carefully. A dollar ninety-one it was with tax. He even had the extra penny ready. And when I asked if he wanted a bag, he still didn't talk. Just shook his head, as if he didn't want me to hear his voice or something. Then, he tucked the bottle carefully into his shirt pocket and walked out."

Silence.

"See, I told you you'd think I was crazy. But with all the trouble up at the big house, I thought—"

"I appreciate your call, Ben. I'll look into it. Thanks very much." He hung up.

"The calm, deliberate way he did everything." What had Dr. Landers said about compulsive cases? They never get upset. They are always calm and deliberate. Even when they are planning a murder? He dialed the doctor's number. Thank God she was in. He asked his question.

"Oh yes. This type of individual would be especially calm and focused when planning a murder. Have you made any progress?"

"Not yet. But I think the case is about to break."

"Good luck," she said.

Close on the tail of that call, the phone rang again.

Doyle. "Something's come up. . . ."

"What . . . ?"

The harsh sound of the Pancoasts' antiquated doorbell carried to Fenimore over the phone line. "Hang on," she said, "I'll be right back."

He fiddled with the phone wire, trying to disentangle it. Sal, thinking it was a game, began batting it with her paw.

"It's the man to read the meter," Doyle said, sounding out of breath. Then she added, in an oddly strained voice, "It's the *first man*."

"What's that?"

They were disconnected.

"What the devil did she mean by that?" he said aloud.

"Is there something wrong, Doctor?"

"Oh, Mrs. Dunwoody—"

"I let myself in," she said. "It's my turn to set up for the class tonight." (Horatio had the ladies well trained.)

"Go right ahead," he said absently.

"Was that Kathleen on the phone? I couldn't help overhearing."

"Yes. We were interrupted by the doorbell. When she came back she said it was the meter man. But then—" Fenimore frowned—"she said a queer thing. She said, with great emphasis, 'It's the *first man.*' Now what do you make of that?"

Mrs. Dunwoody pondered, but only for a moment. "Well, Doctor, to an old Sunday School teacher like myself, the 'first man' will always be—Adam."

Mrs. Doyle turned from the phone to face the man she had just let in. He wore his brown uniform cap pulled low over his forehead, and dark glasses. He carried a notebook in one hand and a heavy flashlight in the other. Around his waist hung a tool belt filled with tools—a hammer, a screwdriver, and—a hatchet.

"Why are you calling so late?" she asked. (It was after 8 P.M.)

He laughed. "With all the women working these days," he said, "it's the only time I can catch anyone at home." He spoke in a hoarse whisper and pointed to his throat. "Laryngitis."

It all sounded plausible.

"Could you show me where it is? I'm new on this job."

Mrs. Doyle gestured to the door at the end of the hall. "That goes to the cellar." But she made no move to accompany him.

"I mean the meter. Could you show me where that is?"

"Sorry. I'm just a guest in the house. I wouldn't know."

"Maybe we could find it together." He moved a step closer.

Mrs. Doyle stepped back. "You take a look. If you can't find it, call me."

"I think I'd find it quicker with your help." He took another step forward and raised the heavy flashlight.

248

CHAPTER 44

After instructing the Seacrest Police to go to the Pancoast house, Fenimore called Rafferty. His friend agreed immediately to place one of the department's helicopters and a pilot at the doctor's disposal. Nearly half the members of the karate class had arrived, but no Horatio. Mrs. Dunwoody explained the situation to her classmates and they eagerly agreed to accompany the doctor. A police van that happened to be cruising in the neighborhood rushed the party, sirens screaming, to the Police Administration Building. The chopper took off from the roof not more than twenty minutes after Mrs. Dunwoody had decoded Mrs. Doyle's message.

Under any other circumstances, the flight would have been an aesthetic experience. The Philadelphia skyline was breathtaking—with its soaring glass buildings—ablaze with light. But these passengers, united by their common fear for Mrs. Doyle's safety, might have been flying over the dark, primeval forest of

William Penn's day, for all the attention they paid the glowing city.

The twenty-minute ride seemed interminable. The bright suburban sprawl of Cherry Hill, followed by the dark fields of corn and soybeans, and finally—the twinkling lights of Seacrest nestled beside the black ocean. As the helicopter descended, its passengers let out a communal sigh.

Following Fenimore's orders, the pilot landed in a field not far from the Pancoast house, hoping the noise of the chopper would not alert Mrs. Doyle's intruder.

"It would be best to take this fellow by surprise," Fenimore warned the ladies as they prepared to disembark.

One by one, they quietly descended and made their way across the field toward the silent house. Several windows were illuminated. Mrs. Dunwoody was the first to press her face to the parlor window. She beckoned to Fenimore.

Seated at a card table, her back to them, was Mrs. Doyle. She seemed to be playing a game of solitaire. On the floor opposite her, leaning against a bookcase, sat a young man. His eyes were closed and he was trussed as neatly as a turkey ready for the oven.

Fenimore, not wanting to alarm his nurse by rapping on the glass, went around to the front door and rang the bell.

Expecting more police, Mrs. Doyle opened the door readily. There was already one policeman in the kitchen waiting for reenforcements to take the prisoner to the police station. She had offered to go with him, but the policeman had looked at her askance.

"Surprise!" Fenimore grinned. "Just thought we'd drop by for a game of gin."

His nurse stared openmouthed.

"I brought along a few of your cronies, in case you needed help, but you seem to have everything under control." He nodded at the bundle by the bookcase.

"Oh, Kathleen, are you all right?" cried Mrs. Dunwoody.

"We were so worried about you," said another octogenarian.

Mrs. Doyle was quite unnerved by the sight of the doctor and her students showing so much concern for her. Her eyes grew moist. Recovering quickly, she demanded, "How on earth did you get here so quickly?"

"A little bird brought us," said Fenimore. He drew her over to the window and pointed to the blue and silver chopper perched in the field, like a giant dragonfly.

"My word! I've always wanted to ride in one of those. Was it fun?"

"It would have been," said Mrs. Dunwoody, "if we hadn't been worried to death about you."

"How did you do it, Kathleen?" The ladies were admiring Mrs. Doyle's karate technique the way another group of women might admire the elaborate icing on a cake or some intricate embroidery stitch.

Mrs. Doyle smiled. "A clean chop to the carotid," she said. "He was about to clobber me with that." She pointed to the flashlight on the card table.

"And the knots," exclaimed one lady, bending over the victim's wrists. "Where did you learn to tie like that?"

"Oh," she blushed. "I have the Navy to thank for that. I did a stint of nursing in the service, you know. Now come on out to the kitchen and have some tea. The police can take care of that." She cast a scornful look at Adam.

The members of the Red Umbrella Brigade trotted eagerly out to the kitchen. When the policeman heard them coming, he decided to wait for his reenforcements outside and ducked out the back door.

Fenimore remained in the parlor. As he stared at the neatly trussed bundle by the bookcase, he was overcome by remorse. How could he face Judith?

CHAPTER 45

When Fenimore met Judith in the dingy reception room of the prison infirmary, she brushed his contrite apologies aside. "No wonder you thought I was a mad killer, Doctor. I must have looked a fright without my wig—grinning up at you in that hysterical way. But I was so upset—seeing Emily and Mrs. Doyle teetering on that balcony, surrounded by smoke and flames—for a moment, I think I did go a little mad."

"Judith—" Fenimore looked at her earnestly. "Tell me one thing. Did you or did you not say to me, 'I almost got them'?"

Judith wrinkled her forehead. "Oh no, Doctor." Her brow cleared. "You must have misunderstood me. What I said was, '*It* almost got them,' meaning the fire, of course." She raised her eyebrows. "Goodness, to think that one little consonant stood between me and the gallows!" (Judith hadn't caught up with the electric chair yet.) "We are all here by a fine thread, aren't we, Doctor?"

Fenimore was silent. A lowercase "t" even resembles a gallows, he thought morosely. The first thing he must do when he got back to Philadelphia was have his hearing checked by a reputable otolaryngologist.

As he took his gracious friend's arm, preparing to lead her outside, he couldn't help apologizing once more for subjecting her to such poor accommodations.

"Nonsense," she said cheerfully, glancing around the ugly little room, "it reminds me of a nursing home. Some of my best friends live in places just like this."

CHAPTER 46

Later, that same day, Fenimore tied up the loose ends of the Pancoast case for Rafferty as they faced each other in a booth at *The Raven*. The dinner was Fenimore's treat—a small gesture of appreciation for the loan of one helicopter.

"Motive!" demanded Rafferty, shaking out his napkin.

"Ah. That was a tough one. And the reason why my suspicions didn't fall on Adam sooner. But he spilled it all out this afternoon when I went to see him. Money—*the love of which* is the root of all evil. He needed big bucks for his special project, or—mission."

"Mission?" Rafferty raised an eyebrow.

"To found a chain of private schools throughout the country which would specialize in the sciences and in which the standard of excellence for entry and graduation would be the highest. Only the best and the brightest would be allowed in—or out."

"Go on." Rafferty was intrigued.

"You see, Adam feared that America was falling behind in the science race. He often attended international conferences on science education and he knew that other countries were providing more rigorous academic training for their young people. England, Japan, and Germany. He wanted to correct that. He visualized the next stage of this country as a great empire— not unlike the Roman Empire. And he thought that our power and influence—our future place in history—would be jeopardized by our mediocre science program."

"Nothing crazy about that—"

"No, but listen—" Fenimore sipped his martini. "Adam taught science at a boys' school which demanded very little of its pupils—except in athletics. And when he tried to raise the standard of excellence in his courses, the administration sat on him—telling him the parents would complain if their little darlings had to stretch their minds too much and made poor grades. This was frustrating to a dedicated teacher who instinctively demanded the best of himself and his students."

"Hmm."

"Adam suspected that many American schools suffered from a similar malaise. So, he came up with this plan to found a chain of schools across the country which would be rigorously academic. But to implement his scheme required money. Piles of it. He knew his wife's family was very wealthy. But he also knew he wouldn't be able to get his hands on it until he was old. By then it might be too late. Too late to save his country. And even then, he would only get a piece of it. His wife's piece. The rest would go to her brother and sister. His wife's piece wouldn't be enough. And he could never make enough as a teacher to increase it significantly. But if he had the whole lot—the entire Pancoast fortune? Now that would be something to work with. And once he had established a sample school, he could apply to the government for grants to create more."

"So, he systematically set about bumping off the Pancoast heirs—" Rafferty downed his martini. "And how was our little fanatic going to explain why *he* wasn't murdered?"

"Oh, but he was murdered. To avert suspicion from himself, he became a murder victim. He drowned—temporarily—in a sailing accident."

"And his resurrection? How did he plan to explain that?"

"Amnesia. He had it carefully planned. He would lie low for a year. He had been preparing for this for a long time—hoarding food and other supplies and stashing them in an abandoned boathouse in a deserted marsh outside of town. It had a cot, a woodstove, and books. Hundreds of books on science, in many different languages, on the latest scientific topics—particle physics, cold fusion, black holes, TOE (the Theory of Everything). He even had a telescope. In his spare time he was an astronomy buff."

"In his spare time? Between murders, you mean?"

"When he rose from the dead," Fenimore went on, "he planned to represent himself as an amnesia victim—the result of a bump on the head from the boom of his boat."

"Why didn't he drown?"

"He came to and hung on to the boat until it reached shore. Then, dazed, he wandered off, unable to remember who he was, where he was . . . and he has been wandering ever since. That was to be his story."

"*Random Harvest II.* Then, one day, he suddenly wakes up, remembers where he lived, his wife, his two kids, and—in this case—all that lovely money!"

"Something like that."

"And he almost got away with it."

"If it hadn't been for Doyle."

"Doyle?"

"She upset his plans. Adam had planned to murder Mildred by drowning her in the bathtub. He was hiding in her bathroom closet, waiting for her. But she never came. Why? Because Mrs. Doyle had interrupted Mildred's schedule by taking her out to tea and then inviting her back to the Pancoast house for dinner. There, Mildred witnessed the preliminary scene for her own murder—a clothespin submerged in the dollhouse bathtub."

"Clothespin?" Rafferty spread his hands. "You've lost me."

Fenimore described the burial of the dolls and the substitution of clothespins by the murderer.

Rafferty ran a hand through his hair and whistled. The mean streets of Philadelphia rarely provided such interesting murderers.

"Mildred ended up in the local sanitarium, which, for Adam's purposes, was almost as good as dead. But it unnerved him. He took a two-month break after that. There were no murders between the end of March and the end of May. I thought he had given up."

"Then there was the fire," Rafferty prompted, after ordering a second martini.

"Right. He decided to do in my nurse along with Judith and Emily Pancoast. Three birds with one conflagration. He owed

258

Doyle one for messing up his plans for Mildred." Fenimore scanned the menu and handed it to his friend. "That was the only time he didn't create a preliminary scene beforehand. He didn't have to. It had already been created for him by the aunts—when they had burned the dollhouse."

"What was the point of setting up those preliminary scenes, anyway? It obviously increased his risk of being caught."

"Ritual. Compulsive ritual. He was an obsessive-compulsive scientist. In the lab, the scientist always tries out his experiments before attempting them in real life. Adam couldn't conceive of killing someone without having a little practice session first. In his twisted mind, the dolls took the place of mice or guinea pigs. When the aunts disposed of them, he substituted clothespins. We found a box of them in his boathouse hideaway. Mildred's attempts to exorcise Seacrest of them was all for naught. And that's not all we found." Fenimore reached in his pocket and placed a small object on the table in front of Rafferty.

"A toy sailboat—" Rafferty picked up the small vessel. No more than three inches high and two inches long, it fit in the palm of his hand.

"It's the one that disappeared from the dollhouse carriage house before Adam's boating accident. I was surprised he hadn't destroyed it. If found, it would have been a piece of incriminating evidence. Then it occurred to me—maybe Adam felt it was a talisman. A sort of good luck charm. As long as it survived, so would he. Maybe he was as superstitious as Mildred. That would explain his great antipathy toward her. We often despise those who share our weaknesses."

"That's something for you and Dr. Landers to work out over lunch," Rafferty grinned. "What I want to know is—why wasn't Adam worried about his wife? Didn't it occur to him that if she was the only Pancoast left, she would inherit all that money and become the primary suspect?"

"Oh, he thought of that. He was very clever. Every time he committed a murder he made sure Susanne had an airtight alibi. When Pamela was poisoned, Susanne was playing charades with the family in the parlor; when Tom was asphyxiated, she was picking up the children at school; when Marie was struck on the head, no one was present and no alibi was needed; and when Edgar was harpooned, Susanne was driving Mrs. Doyle to Mildred's house or helping the aunts make cucumber sandwiches. Her husband's murder would, of course, explain itself when he reappeared. And the night Adam had planned to drown Mildred, he had made sure that his wife was out of town. Susanne had taken the children to a dentist in Ocean City. The appointment had been of long standing and he knew of it before he disappeared. He also knew that after every visit to the dentist, his wife took the children for a treat to a small family restaurant where everybody knew them."

"Okay, okay." Rafferty threw up his hands. "I get it. This guy's a genius. But how did he manage to set up all those little preliminary scenes in the dollhouse without leaving any prints behind? You told me the bathtub was completely clean. So was the bust of Hercules, the harpoon, and the little hatchet."

Fenimore reached in his pocket and pulled out a surgical instrument. It resembled a small pair of scissors, with one difference—although the ends were tapered, they were blunt like tweezers.

"What's that?"

"A hemostat. It's used for a variety of delicate surgical procedures, such as drawing thread through an incision, grabbing a lost sponge—"

"So you *do* lose them?"

Using the hemostat, Fenimore reached for a peanut in the bowl on the table. He removed it deftly, barely disturbing the peanuts on either side.

"Useful," Rafferty admitted. "Wonder why they don't issue them to our boys. Can it pick locks?"

Fenimore grinned. "On occasion."

"But even with that, he still stood a chance of getting caught poking around the dollhouse in plain view of everyone."

"That was where he had an advantage. He knew the aunts' house inside and out. He was their handyman. He fixed their plumbing, solved their electrical problems, and did their carpentry. And the house helped him. Like most Victorian houses, it was full of secret hiding places—closets, cupboards, and back staircases. He knew every one of them. He even used the dumbwaiter to carry his tools from one floor to another. It was the perfect house for his purposes. And, of course, he was familiar with the aunts' habits and schedule. He knew when they went to market, what time they took their naps, and so forth—"

"Okay. Here's the sixty-four-dollar question. Why did he go after Doyle again? There was Judith safely tucked away in prison, ready to take the rap for him—thanks to you."

Fenimore reddened.

"Why didn't he let sleeping dogs lie? He could have easily buggered Emily's pacemaker again—"

Fenimore had recounted that episode to Rafferty earlier. How one night Adam had slipped Emily a sedative, gone into her room after she was asleep, and, with the programmer Fenimore had left behind, reset her pacemaker so it didn't take over when it should have. Since Fenimore had also kindly left the instruction book behind, Adam, an able scientist, had had no problem figuring out the instructions and then lowering the heart rate at which the artificial pacemaker kicked in. Later on, Emily began to have her "spells" and the artificial pacemaker didn't take over when her natural pacemaker slowed up.

"Adam could even have waited for Emily to die of natural causes" Rafferty said. "She was getting on, after all. Why did he risk everything and go after Doyle—who wasn't even an heir?"

Fenimore smiled. "You're the expert on motives, my friend. You tell me."

Rafferty grinned. "Revenge."

"Bingo! He was furious at her for meddling in his affairs. The final blow was when Doyle saved Emily from the fire. He told me so this afternoon, in his calm, deliberate way. When Doyle's name came up, he began arranging four pencils on the desk into a perfect square. He did this over and over again. According to Dr. Landers, this is one way these obsessive-compulsive types demonstrate their rage."

"What did he plan to do with the five kids? They were heirs too. Drown them like kittens?"

"He told me they wouldn't be a problem. He was used to handling children. They'd do what he told them."

"Huh. They must be different from my kids. By the way, what made Doyle suspect him?"

Their waiter was hovering with pad and pencil, but from long experience, knew better than to interrupt *The Raven*'s two best customers.

"When he came to the door that night, posing as a meter man, he attempted to disguise his voice by pretending to have laryngitis. Mrs. Doyle is a nurse. At one time in her career, she was a school nurse. She'd had lots of practice with kids trying to fake illnesses to get out of school. No kid ever got past her. Neither did Adam."

CHAPTER 47

Back in Philadelphia, Mrs. Doyle approached her desk cautiously. Resting on top of her typewriter was a small package, tastefully wrapped in pink tissue paper and tied with white satin ribbon. She was not accustomed to receiving gifts at eight o'clock in the morning. Or at any other time, for that matter. Dr. Fenimore was nowhere to be seen.

As if expecting it to explode, she ripped off the wrappings and stood a safe distance away while observing the contents. A small white jewelry box. Warily, she lifted the lid. Inside, on a bed of cotton, lay a delicate brooch. It was in the shape of an umbrella, made of gold and—

"Garnets, Doyle." Fenimore stood in the doorway. "I couldn't spring for rubies."

She took out the brooch and pinned it to the lapel of her freshly starched uniform.

"I thought you deserved something—" he mumbled.

"Oh, Doctor—" Ferociously, she attacked a pile of Medicare forms.

This touching scene was followed by a not so touching one. Horatio arrived and learned that he had missed a helicopter ride by five minutes.

"But we couldn't wait," Fenimore explained. "It was an emergency."

"Five minutes!"

"We didn't know you would be only five minutes and we thought Mrs. Doyle's life was in danger."

Horatio scowled at the nurse.

The nurse smiled complacently.

CHAPTER 48

Maybe I'm wrong," Fenimore said.

He and Jennifer were in her apartment enjoying a final glass of wine at the end of a pleasant evening. Jennifer had made dinner and she and her father and Fenimore had talked about books and watched *Spellbound*, starring Ingrid Bergman and Gregory Peck. Fenimore had requested that film because he had wanted to compare Peck's behavior with Adam's.

A few minutes earlier, Mr. Nicholson had excused himself and retired with a book under each arm—one in Latin and one in Greek. They had laughed about that, and sat in easy silence sipping their wine, until Fenimore had made his remark.

"What do you mean?" asked Jennifer.

"Maybe I'm wrong about this whole medical business. Insisting on practicing solo. Working alone. Maybe teams *are* better. Maybe they get more done. Save more lives. Get more people well."

Jennifer set down her glass and looked at him.

"Well, I was wrong about Judith. Maybe I'm wrong about this too."

"Anyone can make a mistake."

"But what a mistake! Do you realize she could have gone to prison for life?" He set his glass down next to hers. "She was so depressed by all the deaths in the family, she didn't even protest. What could I have been thinking of? She had no motive. I knew that. But I just barreled along. I was so tired of the case, so sick of it, so anxious to close it, I jumped at the first opportunity to accuse somebody. And Judith—of all people!" He stood up and began to pace, continuing his soliloquy. "If I'd had a partner or a group to consult with they might have stopped me, urged me to reconsider, made other—better suggestions. But no, I had to do it all by myself. Perfect Andrew knows all the answers." He paused to look down at her. "And I was wrong. Dead wrong."

"That doesn't mean you'll be wrong the next time, or the time after that. And you've often been right. Look at your past record. Besides," Jennifer went on, "you did consult Rafferty. And he was the one who set you on the wrong track. He was the one who suggested that one of the Pancoast sisters might be guilty."

"And was I ever suggestible!" He stopped pacing.

"It works both ways," Jennifer continued. "Teammates and consultants can give bad advice as well as good."

He sat down beside her.

"You can't suddenly decide that the individual is worthless because of one isolated case."

He took her hand.

"And Judith *has* forgiven you."

He pulled her close.

The question really was, could he forgive himself?

CHAPTER 49

Where is 'Pomp and Circumstance'?" asked Mrs. Dòyle, frantically.

"On the Main Line," said Fenimore.

"No, I mean the tape. We need it for the ceremony."

Fenimore scrabbled through the box of dusty casette tapes at his elbow and came up with it. "Here." He handed it to her.

She rushed off to attend to some other urgent duty.

The graduation of the karate class was to take place at one o'clock and there was still much to be done. The punch and cookies were in the kitchen. Jennifer had donated her punch bowl and a ladle. Horatio had swept out and hosed down the cellar. An enormous bouquet of old-fashioned yellow roses decked the hot water heater. This arrangement was a gift from the Pancoast sisters, who had sent their regrets, feeling that a long trip in the heat would be too much for Emily.

The diplomas were nestled in a basket on a card table set up at one end of the cellar. In front of the table, twenty-five folding chairs were lined up, in rows of five each. Guests and well-wishers would have to stand along the walls, as there were no more chairs.

"Where are the fuckin' umbrellas?" Horatio was nervous because he had been pressed into taking part in the ceremony.

"They're up here," called a muffled voice from above.

"Well, bring them down for Chrissake!"

There was a dragging, thumping noise.

"Hold on." Horatio rushed up the stairs to help Mrs. Doyle with the heavy cartons of red umbrellas.

By twelve forty-five all the graduates and their guests were miraculously assembled. Jennifer had even brought her father, to swell the crowd. And Fenimore had badgered some of the neighbors to come. The neighbors on either side of Fenimore's house had needed no persuasion. They were curious to see who had caused all those mysterious thumps and shouts during the past six months.

Mrs. Doyle had written a speech, and Horatio, under duress, had agreed to hand out the diplomas and the umbrellas. "Do I have to say anything?" he asked, anxiously.

"God, no," Fenimore said quickly.

The boy looked relieved.

As the first strains of "Pomp and Circumstance" filtered from the tape player, the ladies, clad in their customery karate attire—red leotards and black belts—took their places one by one. Mrs. Doyle, in her role as mistress of ceremonies, wore a simple navy blue suit. Its only adornment—a charming brooch in the shape of an umbrella. She cleared her throat:

"Today I would like to welcome this year's graduates of the karate class—"

Wild applause.

"—otherwise known as the Red Umbrella Brigade—or RUB."

More applause.

When her speech was finished, the graduates-to-be lined up to receive their awards. As Mrs. Doyle read off their names and they each stepped up, Horatio slapped a diploma in one hand and shoved a red umbrella in the other. After the last graduate had returned to her seat and the applause had died down, Mrs. Doyle made an announcement: "Since Dr. Fenimore so kindly lent us these premises for our classes, we'd like to present him with a small token of our appreciation."

Everyone looked at the doctor. He blushed.

"Please step up, Doctor."

Acutely embarrassed, he shuffled forward. Mrs. Doyle handed him a beautifully wrapped package about the size and shape of a shoe box.

Fenimore mumbled, "Thank you," and hurried back to his spot against the wall.

Later, when they had retired upstairs for refreshments, the graduates and guests gathered around the doctor to watch him open his present. He pulled off the wrappings to reveal what was—in fact—a shoe box. He lifted the lid. There lay a pair of the most beautiful, top-of-the-line, brand-name sneakers. Lifting one out, he held it up for everyone to see.

"Cool," came from Horatio in the rear.

"I am overwhelmed," Fenimore said. "Now I can never give up my fitness classes!"

Much laughter.

As Fenimore sipped punch and nibbled cookies with Jennifer and her father, Jennifer said, "What's going to become of your kamikazi sneakers?"

"Oh, I'll keep them around for emergencies," Fenimore said.

"Such as?"

"A leak in the roof or a flood in the cellar. I wouldn't want to soil those beautiful, state-of-the-art specimens with tar or water." He grinned.

Mr. Nicholson broke in, "I'm sorry I couldn't find that eighteenth-century French medical text you were looking for. . . ."

"Oh, don't worry about it."

"I'm sure Jennifer would have found a copy for you," her father continued, "if she hadn't cut her trip short. When she walked in the door a month early, you could have knocked me over with a feather."

Fenimore looked at Jennifer.

Jennifer looked at her punch.

RALPH McINERNY'S
NOTRE DAME MYSTERIES

In each of these acclaimed mysteries, the brilliant Knight brothers—a detective and a philosophy professor—must scour the Notre Dame campus for a ruthless killer and score a goal for justice.

"Wonderful . . . Give McInerny a few more entries, and he'll have readers comparing the Knight brothers with the best detective duos in the genre."

—Booklist

ON THIS ROCKNE
Bodies pile up as the stage is set for a 10-million-dollar memorial to legendary Notre Dame football coach Knute Rockne.

LACK OF THE IRISH
The mysterious death of a campus administrator threatens to steal the headlines at the big football game between Catholic Notre Dame and Protestant Baylor University.

IRISH TENURE
When the body of a female philosophy professor is found in a freezing lake, the suspects include a rejected would-be suitor, a rare-book dealer and a rival for tenure. Who on campus would take academic rivalry to murderous new heights?

In all of New York's Chinatown, there is no one
like P.I. Lydia Chin, who has a nose for trouble,
a disapproving Chinese mother, and a partner
named Bill Smith who's been living above a bar
for sixteen years.

Hired to find some precious stolen porcelain,
Lydia follows a trail of clues from highbrow art
dealers into a world of Chinese gangs.
Suddenly, this case has become as complex as
her community itself—and as deadly as a killer
on the loose...

China Trade

S. J. Rozan

CT 1/99

READ THE ONLY MYSTERY THAT WON BOTH
THE EDGAR AND SHAMUS AWARDS!

A COLD DAY
IN PARADISE

STEVE HAMILTON

Other than the bullet lodged less than a centimeter from his heart, former Detroit police officer Alex McKnight thought he had put the nightmare of his partner's death and his own near-fatal injury behind him. After all, Maximilian Rose, convicted of the crimes, has been locked in the state pen for years. But in the small town of Paradise, Michigan, where McKnight has traded his badge for a cozy cabin in the woods, a murderer with Rose's unmistakable trademarks appears to be back to his killing ways. And it seems as if it will be a frozen day in hell before McKnight can unravel the cold truth from a deadly deception in a town that's anything but Paradise.

AVAILABLE WHEREVER BOOKS ARE SOLD
FROM ST. MARTIN'S PAPERBACKS

CDP 12/99